T

Kingdom

of Argon

By

M.J. INNES

For my own family of goblins

One

Our story begins on a frosty Sunday night, the third Sunday in November. In an ordinary house, on an ordinary street within an ordinary village, something extraordinary was just about to take place.

Two children lay in bed, exhausted after a busy weekend. Jack on the top bunk with Codie on the bottom. Their dad had just finished that night's chapter of the latest David Walliams book. Jack was as snug as a bug in a rug, Codie, however, was not quite as content as their father kissed the boys goodnight and made his way out of the room.

A NOISE.

'Jack? Jack? Did you hear that?' Codie said, his eyes poking out from beneath his thick, navy duvet.

'I didn't hear anything. Go to sleep!' Jack replied, growing irritated with his brother's familiar bedtime antics.

A GENTLE BANG FROM THE OPPOSITE END OF THE ROOM.

'You must have heard that?' Codie pleaded.

Jack sat up in bed, frustrated with his younger sibling. Was he this annoying when he was seven?

'How many times? We go through this every night. There is nobody here. Nobody at the window, nobody in the hall and **NOBODY** in the wardrobe! Now please, can you just close your eyes so we can get a decent night's sleep for once?'

Silence filled the air, then...

A THUNDERING BANG SOUNDED FROM THE OPPOSITE END OF THE ROOM.

Before Codie had a chance to speak, his brother shot up in bed once more.

'I heard it that time.' Jack said, throwing his covers off and climbing down the ladder from the top bunk. For a moment the boy stood perfectly still on the floor, glaring into the darkness.

BANG!

Jacks eyes darted to the corner of the bedroom where the boys' wardrobe stood. He reached out and tapped his brother's leg without taking his eyes off the wardrobe. 'Codie,' he whispered, before turning to look at his brother, who was now completely concealed by his duvet.

5

ANOTHER BANG.

Jack launched himself into Codie's bed, pulling more than his fair share of duvet over himself. Both brothers lay perfectly still, Jack thought about turning the bedroom light on but daren't move, eyes fixated on the wardrobe at the far end of the room.

Jack lay perfectly still, frantically biting his nails as a minute of silence passed. And then another. By the time the third minute had lapsed Jack was beginning to feel slightly foolish. Had he imagined it? Maybe all Codie's fussing had finally fuelled him with panic.

This was silly. He thought about calling down to his dad but as any self-respecting ten-year-old boy knows, bravery comes at a price.

'What's in there?' Codie said eventually.

6

Jack waited for another moment, then decided this was childish. There was nothing and no one there. He had a big football match after school tomorrow and he knew he needed a good night's sleep if he was going to wipe the smug smile off Jason McCann's face.

Jack shook his head before tossing the covers back over his brother. He slowly stood up, looked into Codie's worried brown eyes, and assured him that it was just his imagination and that he should try to get some sleep.

Just as Jack was about to mount the ladder back up to his bed, a nerve-jangling noise made him freeze on the ground. It was the sound of the wardrobe door opening.

* *

Jack tentatively turned to face the wardrobe, unsure what was going to greet him.

The boys had a one-year-old Syrian hamster called Nibbles. He could always be counted on to be getting up to some kind of mischief once the curtains were closed. But it couldn't be Nibbles; he was downstairs having the time of his life, no doubt with both pouches full of goodies.

Jack stole a brief glance at Codie, who now looked absolutely terrified, before he focused once again on the wardrobe.

He could make out a thick, chubby hand in the darkness of their room. For some reason none of the boys screamed, more out of shock than bravery this time.

A second hand appeared, this one just as chubby as the last, before two feet plumped down on the ground. Jack instinctively moved in front of his brother's bed, attempting to shield him from what was to come.

With a great heaving sound, whatever it was pulled itself up and out of the wardrobe.

The first thing Jack noticed was the size of its ears. Great long, pointed ears as it turned and looked at him. Jack could only just make out the outline of its face through the darkness before it stirred and sauntered directly over to him, kicking over a small chest of Codie's toys in the process.

Jack cringed at the horror of what greeted him. Its pudgy, pale face was alarming - grotesque even, with long jet-black shaggy hair and a small red hat atop. Its only soothing feature was big black, affectionate eyes.

The boys stayed still, fixed to the ground.

The interloper was now only centimetres away from Jack. It was slightly taller than he was and Jack may have imagined it, but he was pretty sure a whiff of pickled onions had filled the room.

The intruder took another step forward before saying something Jack truly didn't expect. 'You lot got any breakfast going or what?'

'I'm sorry?' said Jack, gawking at the creature. Its accent was strange and mysterious. Jack had to run through the question twice in his head before it resembled a sentence.

'It seems like a perfectly reasonable thing to ask for after twelve hours kip.'

'No, my mum doesn't usually make it until morning,' Jack said, rubbing his eyes, just to make sure he wasn't dreaming.

'Hmm' said the intruder, belching loudly and scratching its bottom simultaneously.

'How did you get in here?'

'I climbed. Right up that window there.' The creature pointed to the window in the bedroom.

'But the window's locked.'

'Ways and means my little friend, ways and means.'

Jack took a step forward, feeling slightly calmer than he had been a moment ago. 'Why are you here?'

This time it was the creature's turn to inch forward, copying the boy, now only millimetres from Jack's face, before it whispered: 'I'm hiding, I am.'

'Hiding from what?'

'Em Er, I can't tell you that.'

'Why not?'

'If I tell you, I'll be putting you in all kinds of danger.'

Jack reached over his shoulder and turned the small night light on.

'Ok, so let me get this straight,' Jack said, sounding more courageous than he felt. 'You break into our house, sleep for twelve hours in our wardrobe and,' Jack paused for a moment, 'is that my dad's favourite cardigan you're wearing?'

'I was cold,' the creature replied sheepishly, 'plus it smelled like home.'

Jack shook his head in disbelief. 'I see. Well, I think it's about time for you to leave. My brother and I' (Jack stepped aside to reveal Codie) 'have to get up very early for school in the morning and we can't have some monster hiding in our bedroom.'

The creature stood up straight.

'My name is Henry. Henry Xavier Gryphon Bagwell and I sir, am a goblin.'

'Goblins aren't real, everybody knows that.'

'Course we're real! If we goblins aren't real, then explain to me how I can be standing in front of you mister?'

Got me there, Jack thought, as he pieced together the goblin's strange dialect.

'Aren't goblins bad?' Codie asked, finally feeling brave enough to speak.

'We goblins have been given a bad name by you homins.'

'It's humans,' Jack corrected.

'Is it?' Henry said with an enormous smile. 'Most of us goblins are nice folk whose only desire is to live peacefully. But there is a small amount of... bad apples.'

Jack drummed his fingers on the windowsill. 'So, I guess it's one of these bad apples that you're hiding from?'

'The baddest apple.'

'Baddest?' Jack chuckled, struggling to take it all in. 'So, what does this "baddest apple" want with you?'

Henry thought for a moment then looked over at the smallest child, who was yawning. 'Your brother's tired. He needs some sleep I'd reckon. Tell you what, if you'd be so kind as

13

to let me kip in that wonderful chest of yours until your sun comes up, I'll be on my way.'

Jack looked at Codie, who in all honesty looked exhausted. 'Fair enough' Jack relented, still coming to terms with the fact that a goblin was having a sleepover at his house. If he told anyone at school about this in the morning, they'd think he was bonkers!

Codie lay down in bed, almost asleep before his head hit the pillow. As if a slumber party with a peculiar goblin was par for the course.

Without so much as another word, Henry trudged over to the wardrobe and heaved himself back inside, his plump, stumpy fingers reaching out and pulling the doors closed with a creak.

Jack climbed the ladder and got back into bed. Surprisingly, sleep came easily enough for him, too. Perhaps he would have taken longer to drift off if he knew exactly what Henry Xavier Gryphon Bagwell had in store for the two boys the following day.

Two

Jack woke with a jump. He rubbed his eyes. Was it morning? It felt like morning but it was hard to tell with the dark winter gloom he could detect from between his bedroom curtains. He thought for a moment, glaring up at the pale white ceiling and running a hand over his short, brown, spikey hair. He heaved himself out of bed and down the metal ladder, glancing at the clock fixed to the wall before landing firmly on the bedroom carpet.

He stretched loudly. 'Codie you will never believe the dream I had last...' But before Jack could finish his sentence, he heard a somewhat familiar voice, the same voice that had given him and Codie such a scare during the night.

Jack looked into Codie's bed; he could barely believe his eyes. There was Henry the goblin, bold as brass -, plumped on Codie's bed, reading a chapter of Zog - Codie's favourite book. His brown tattered trousers had slipped up a couple of inches at the bottom, revealing one white sock and one black sock held in place by a pair of ghastly brown sandals. And he was still proudly donning Dad's favourite cardigan. Codie looked as if he had been up for hours. His sandy brown hair was normally wild first thing in the morning. But not today, it looked tidy - possibly even brushed.

'Still here I see?' Jack said awkwardly.

Henry looked up at the boy with a smile. 'I was just about to leave, but then this little fella asked if I could read him a quick chapter. Glad I did too, cracking read it is.'

'Right, well we need to get downstairs for breakfast. I'm not sure how mum and dad would feel knowing we allowed a goblin to stay the night.'

'Ah, right you are. We're gonna have to leave it there,' Henry said, nonchalantly sliding the book into his pocket for later and leaping off the bed.

'I'm going to need my dad's cardigan back too I'm afraid,' Jack said, almost feeling guilty.

Henry bashfully tugged the cardigan up over his head revealing a podgy tummy. As he did, a small shiny box no bigger than a family sized chocolate bar fell out of his trouser pocket, instantly grabbing the attention of both boys.

'What's that?' Jack and Codie blurted out at exactly the same time.

'It's nothing. Pretend you never seen it.' Henry said, as he hastily bent down and carefully picked up the silver box.

Jack couldn't help but stare. Admittedly the box was fairly small, but it was utterly mesmerising, polished, dazzling silver. There was some kind of writing down either end of the box, which from Jack's angle looked to be glowing golden against the silver background. Neither child had ever seen anything like it before.

'What is it?' Jack asked again, as Codie perched himself high up on his bed to get a better look.

Henry sighed, unsure. Then he whispered, 'It's a Tempus Tarda.'

'It's a what?' Codie screeched.

'A Tempus Tarda.'

'I've never heard of such a thing,' Jack said.

'Well of course *you* haven't,' Henry gasped, clearly offended. 'We goblins are extremely careful with our possessions. It would be a pretty foolish goblin to leave the most powerful creation in our world lying around for you homins to find.'

Jacks eyes were fixed on the box. 'Can I hold it?'

Henry shook his head vigorously. 'No! I don't think that's such a good idea. This may just look like a silver box but it's very valuable and extremely dangerous in the wrong hands. If the King ever found out I'd even shown it to homins, I'd, I'd - well let's just say I'd be in a lot of trouble. A lot more trouble, in fact.'

'Is it moving?' asked Codie.

'Moving, no, it's not moving. It's beating.'

'Beating?' Jack said. 'Like a heart?'

'Exactly like a heart.'

'Why have you got it?'

'Not sure if I should be telling you that either. It's goblin business.'

'Come on you can trust us,' Codie said, reaching over and putting his hand on the goblin's shoulder.

Henry stood perfectly still, thinking.

'Come on,' Jack pleaded. 'We let you stay here last night – free of charge. How many other kids would have allowed a goblin to sleep over, and in such beautiful accommodation.' Jack indicated the tired wardrobe at the far end of the room.

'Ok, I'll tell you, but before I do, I must ask you a favour. I wouldn't ask ordinarily, but as you can probably tell I've found myself at a bit of a loose end.'

'We'll do it!' Codie declared excitedly, bouncing widely on the bottom bunk.

'I haven't told you what it is yet! It will be extremely dangerous.'

The bouncing stopped and Codie's face dropped.

Jack put his foot on the first step of the ladder and crossed his arms over his knee. 'Tell you what, you tell us what this favour is, and if it's doable, we'll do all we can to help you.'

Henry eyed the children's excited faces before relenting, 'I need you to help me return this,' Henry held up the Tempus Tarda, 'to its rightful owner.'

'Who is its rightful owner?' Jack asked.

Before Henry could answer, a loud call echoed through the room.

'JACK! CODIE! BREAKFAST!' The children's mother shouted from the bottom of the stairs.

'Hold that thought. You wait here,' Jack said to Henry. 'Me and Codie will pop downstairs, wolf down our breakfast and we'll be right with you, ok?'

'I'm sure I can handle that,' Henry said proudly.

The boys made their way over to the bedroom door.

'You wouldn't happen to have any pickled onions going spare, would you?' Henry asked as politely as he could muster.

'It's quarter to eight in the morning!'

'I know. But like my grandfather, Ellister, used to say, it's never too early for pickled onions.'

Jack and Codie each gave Henry a bizarre look. 'We'll see what we can do,' said Jack.

The boys made their way downstairs, leaving the mischievous goblin alone in their bedroom. The children's mother was happily humming a song to herself as she unloaded the dishwasher.

As usual, Dad had already left for work, while Sallie, their little sister, was sitting in her high chair, face covered in food. At least she isn't crying again, Jack thought. She'd taken her first steps the previous night.

'Ten months old and walking, we have yet another genius in the family,' their father had declared.

The boys each took a seat at the table and hungrily tucked into their breakfast. As usual, Jack had his favourite cereal, Loopty Lous, with a cup of milk next to his bowl – fussy! Codie had his favourite, Choco Pops, flooded with milk.

Within minutes their bowls were empty and, after a quick conversation with their mother, during which, the children promised to get ready for school, they sprinted back upstairs as quickly as their legs would carry them. Both of them desperate to find out more about the Tempus Tarda.

Three

The boys came to a stuttering halt outside the bedroom door. Their hearts were pounding from sprinting up the stairs. Just as they were about to enter, Jack held his hand up. 'Wait!'

The boys put their ears up against the door and listened to the muffled sound of Henry's voice.

'It's ok, don't worry. I trust them, and you will just have to trust me.'

Without giving Henry any warning, Jack and Codie bounced into the room. 'Who are you talking to?' Jack asked.

'Em, no one.' Henry sputtered. 'How'd you get on with those pickled onions?' He obviously wanted to change the subject.

Jack moved aside and Codie produced a large jar of silverskin pickled onions. He'd managed to grab them while their mum had been feeding Sallie one of her many bottles of baby milk. 'You're lucky; these are Dad's favourites. There were a few jars tucked away in the cupboard.'

Henry's eyes lit up, he moved towards the jar and gratefully accepted it.

In one swift motion, the goblin unscrewed the jar, and began drinking the contents. Within ten seconds, and after some very uncomfortable gulping noises, Henry had consumed the entire jar, vinegar and all. He stood perfectly still for a moment, while Jack and Codie watched on. A rumbling which sounded as if it had come from the soles of Henry's feet sounded, before he let out an enormous belch, and his hat flew off his head for a good five seconds.

Jack and Codie looked on in astonishment.

Henry gave his chin a wipe with the back of his pudgy hand, before carrying on as if nothing had happened. 'Now, where were we?'

The boys remained silent for a split second, taking in what they had just seen, then Jack blinked.

'You were about to tell us why you need our help returning that Tempus... whatever it's called, to its owner.'

'Ah, right you are.'

Silence filled the room.

'Well go on then!' Jack prompted, helping himself to a seat on Codie's bed.

Henry walked over to the bedroom door and closed it tight, before turning and facing the two boys. Codie was standing by the window at the opposite end of the room, each of the children waiting patiently for the goblin to enlighten them.

'It all started 20 years ago, although tensions had been growing for years. In my Kingdom, we have two types of goblins: the Trovers and the Yems. I myself am a Trover,' Henry said, pressing a hand against his chest. 'For many years the Yems and the Trovers lived in peace and harmony. Sure, there was the odd disagreement, but generally all was well. Then, gradually, things started to turn. King Gola, leader of the Yems died, well some say he died, I personally believe he was killed.'

'Killed? Who'd want to kill a king?' Jack asked, sitting up straight.

Henry made a cross face at him, before continuing.

'When King Gola died, our lot were very upset. He had done so much over the years to keep the peace between the Trovers and the Yems, we knew it was going to spell trouble.

Plus, he was so young, no one in the Kingdom could quite believe he was gone.'

'How old was he?' Codie interrupted.

Henry clasped his teeth together and made a whistling sound. 'He was only 147.'

'Really?'

'Just a baby when you think about it.'

Jack laughed. 'Is that young for a goblin?'

'It certainly is my little friend. I knew a goblin once that lived until he was 310. Sure his body was in bits but his mind was as quick as someone of 200.'

Henry nostalgically gazed out of the bedroom window for a moment before asking the children, somewhat confused: 'Where was I?'

'You were telling us about this King Gola.'

'I know I know,' Henry said, irritated at losing his train of thought.

The goblin rubbed his temples for a moment before continuing.

'Sure, King Gola, was a Yem but no goblin was ever perfect. He was loved, cherished; I'd go so far as to say he was a hero - even in our Trovers' eyes! Goblins throughout the Kingdom expected him to live forever. The day the King died, there was a bleak realisation that for us goblins, nothing would ever be the same again. His son, Prince James, was only 15 when his father perished and not old enough to rule our land.' Henry was speaking flatly, as if the trauma was still raw. 'Instead an agreement was reached that King Gola's brother, Geerah, would be crowned ruler until Prince James came of age.'

The two boys listened intently, as Henry pushed on with his story.

'That resolution was abolished however, when Geerah got a taste of power. When

Prince James turned 18, his uncle turned on him, telling all in the land that new information had been handed into the crown, which proved that Prince James had killed his father.'

The children looked shocked.

'For obvious reasons, the proof has never been made accessible to the wider audience, mainly because it doesn't exist. But Geerah claimed that the evidence submitted was indisputable.' He even claimed that the king had been poisoned. The following day, Geerah sentenced the young prince to death for treason.'

Codie gasped. 'That's not a very nice thing to do.'

'Indeed it's not, my little friend. But Geerah is not a very nice goblin. He didn't hang around either, immediately ordering his Yemars to kill Prince James that very night!'

31

Jack scrunched his face up into a ball. 'Yemars?'

Henry nodded, cupping his hand around his mouth and nose. 'Ten of the fiercest goblins alive, whose sole aim in life is to protect the king. If only they still had their founding members to guide them.'

There was a loud thump at the bedroom window as a small blackbird flew directly into it. Henry jumped about a foot in the air. Jack and Codie giggled as the goblin composed himself.

'Now, nobody knows how he did it, my guess is some goblin tipped him off, but when the fearsome Yemars went to apprehend Prince James - he was gone. And not so much as a glimpse of Prince James has been seen in the Kingdom since that night!'

'Apparently,' Henry continued. 'When the Yemars went to capture the Prince, they found evidence that he had been assisted in his escape, by a Trover. Nobody knows who this elusive Trover is, but Geerah has certainly made us lot pay for it. Ever since that day, he developed an unhealthy dislike for Trovers, considering us lot to be inferior to the mighty Yems.'

'So where do you think the Prince went?' Jack asked

'No goblin knows for sure. Geerah's followers have scoured our entire land but no trace of Prince James has ever been found.'

Four

The brothers were so engrossed in Henry's story that they neglected to hear their mother trundling her way up the stairs, towards their bedroom. The first they heard of her was when she pulled the handle down and appeared at the bedroom door.

'Jack! Codie! Get a move on! School starts in twenty minutes. What have you two been doing in here?'

Jack gave his eyes a rub. Where on earth did Henry go? One minute he was standing in the middle of the bedroom, the next he was gone.

A somewhat perplexed, Jack, accepted his school uniform from his mum's outstretched arm. Her cheeks were red and her hands were fixed to her hips, as she glowered, unimpressed at her children.

'Sorry,' Jack said. 'I was... em. I was just showing Codie something, something really cool, although it appears to have vanished all of a sudden.'

'That's right,' Codie agreed. He too looked around the bedroom for the missing goblin.

The boy's mother eyed them suspiciously. She opened her mouth to speak as an eruption of sobbing sounding from the somewhere in the house. 'Get dressed; you need to leave for school in ten minutes,' Mum said, as she exited the bedroom.

'Phew! Perfect timing Sallie,' Jack said, as he closed the bedroom door. By the time he had turned around, Henry was back in the centre of the room, with a brazen look on his chubby face.

'Where did you come from?' Jack asked, utterly dumbfounded.

'Can you show me how you did that?' Codie said, scratching his head.

'No, I'm afraid I can't, strictly on a need to know basis, and unfortunately for you two, you don't need to know right now. Now, do you want to hear the rest of my story before school or what?'

'Try and stop me,' Jack said, throwing his newly ironed school uniform on the bottom bunk and jumping back onto the bed himself.

Henry cleared his throat. 'Many years have passed with King Geerah at the helm and times have certainly changed since his brother's harmonious reign. Geerah has constructed a 100-foot-high wall between the north and south of the Kingdom, with any Trovers found in the north being 'faded out' as he calls it.

All of the best jobs in the land are given to Yems, whether they're qualified or not. All the hard, punishing jobs are set aside for Trovers, and the pay for a Trover is capped at 50 buckles a week, which believe me, is nowhere near enough to survive on.

'That's terrible,' Jack said.

'That's not the half of it,' said Henry. 'There are raids carried out on homes of Trovers every other night. Anyone suspected of having any allegiance to Prince James is left with an enormous flag poking out of their chimney. The official flag of the Yems, all purple with a black Y in the middle. What's worse is that any family with the flag fixed into their chimney, seems to mysteriously disappear shortly after. Prison, forced labour or worse.' Henry paused momentarily to catch his breath. 'That's not even the worst part.'

'What's the worst part?' Codie asked, looking terrified.

'Maybe we should leave it there for just now?' Jack said, slightly concerned with how graphic Henry's story was becoming. 'Anyway, none of this explains why you have that Tempus, whatever it's called.'

'It doesn't?' Henry said, looking puzzled. 'Well then I'll tell you! Several months ago, Geerah, and his legions of goblins journeyed into the heart of the south. Apparently, they'd received word that a group of Trovers were growing tired of his awful reign, and that a coup was underway.'

Codie scratched his head. 'What's a coup?'

'It's when a group or army try to overthrow the King,' Jack told him, proud of himself. At school, he'd recently been learning about Napoleon Bonaparte's exploits at the end of the 18th century. 'It's actually how Ms Ratch has climbed so high up the teaching ladder,' he chuckled.

Henry nodded in agreement, although he had no idea who Ms Ratch was. 'Geerah's legions crossed bridges, marched through villages and even crossed the ferocious Lagoon Lake, until they arrived at Trovers Grove. His legions wasted no time in carrying out searches on the many caves scattered throughout the grove. Geerah had expected to catch the group of Trovers off-guard, but it was he himself who was left surprised. There was only one thing in the cave that day and it wasn't a Trover.'

'What was it?' the boys asked simultaneously

'It was a Kobold, by the name of Berke. Kobolds are fascinating magical creatures, but by blue mist, you don't want to get on the wrong side of one. It doesn't matter how many goblins you have in your legions, ain't nobody wants to cross a Kobold. They have ties directly back to Argon himself!'

Jacks eyes widened. 'So what did Geerah do?'

Henry exhaled, 'It didn't stop old Geerah, he thought he was untouchable. Filled with power, he backed Berke into the rear of the cave, trapping the poor Kobold. Without allowing Berke an opportunity to defend himself, Geerah killed the Kobold there and then; little did he realise what a big mistake he was making.'

Jack let out a deep breath, while Codie couldn't hide the shocked look from his face.

'Upon his death,' continued Henry. 'Berke, relinquished all of his possessions; they quite literally came flooding out of him. Gold, silver, jewellery, you name it. One of his possessions however caught the eye of Geerah more than anything else. Can you guess what that was?'

Henry slapped a hand down on the boys' chest of drawers, while reaching into his pocket with the other, 'Exactly!' Henry declared, before the children had a chance to answer. The goblin lifted the Tempus Tarda aloft. 'A Tempus Tarda cannot be taken by force. Inside this little box is something beyond what any of us goblins can begin to comprehend. One thing I do know however, no good ever came from crossing a Kobold.'

'So how is it that you have it?' Jack queried, hoping the niggling suspicion at the back of his mind was wrong.

'Well,' started Henry, 'at least now you're asking some meaty questions. But... I think that's a story for later.' He nodded his head towards Codie.

'Do you still want our help returning the Tempus Tarda?' Jack asked.

'I do. I may come across as an extremely brave, not to mention fetchingly handsome goblin, but I'm scared, and I can't do this alone.'

Jack and Codie looked at each other, both brothers seemingly thinking the same thing.

'We'll do it!' Jack said, jumping up from the bottom bunk. 'But can it wait until after school?'

Henry looked at his wrist. Although he wasn't wearing a watch, that didn't stop him reaching an answer. 'I'm afraid not, if you want to come, we must leave right away!'

'What about school?' Codie asked.

Henry waved a chunky hand and let out a gust of wind from his mouth. 'Don't worry about that. You two get your school uniforms on, I will take care of the rest.'

Within five minutes, the boys were dressed, Jack wearing his usual black trousers, white polo shirt and navy jumper, Codie, was dressed in exactly the same, except his jumper was grey. Both jumpers displayed the familiar badge of Lakewood Primary. The boys brushed their teeth, cleaned their faces and were ready to hit the road.

'You sure you want to do this?' Jack asked Codie as they made their way back into their bedroom.

His brother nodded excitedly.

'I'm grateful, don't get me wrong,' Henry said. 'But it could get very dangerous; I can easily drop you off at school instead?'

It was Jack's turn to jest. 'What and let you have all the fun, no way.'

'As long as you're sure,' said Henry.

The boys gave each other one last look before nodding excitedly at one another.

'Ok,' Henry said. 'You two head downstairs, just like any other day. I'll meet you outside.'

'How are you going to get out of the house?' Jack asked.

Henry tapped his nose twice. 'Ways and means my little friend.'

Jack and Codie hurried downstairs. Their school was no more than a couple of minutes away and they only had one road to cross.

Since Sallie had been born, Mum had started letting the boys walk to school by themselves, which worked out pretty well given their current predicament.

The boys grabbed their school bags, and made sure their jackets, hats and gloves were on securely before giving their mother a kiss goodbye, and leaving their cosy house.

Five

The sky outside was a horrible grey colour while a strong gale was blowing hard in every direction. Jack hated the cold. Actually, he despised the cold. It was the absolute worst thing about living in Scotland. Dark, gloomy, dreich winter mornings. No wonder getting out of bed was such a struggle. Why couldn't he have been born someplace warm, where the sun shone from morning until night, and you didn't need streetlights on before you'd had your breakfast.

Last winter Jack had tried to convince his dad to build a tunnel from their front door to the entrance of his school. The tunnel would have been thermal-insulated to keep the heat in and would have had numerous radiators, no more than one meter apart, each of them on

45

full blast 24 hours a day. Sadly his dad hadn't been convinced.

The brothers began their familiar journey to school. Along the pavement they trundled, every few paces looking back at their mother. As usual, she was stood at the front door waving with one hand while holding Sallie with the other.

Out of the corner of his eye, Jack saw old Mrs Ainslie, the neighbour of two doors up. As was the case with most mornings, she was peering out of her living room window, taking it all in. As usual, her cat Toby, was in her arms eyeing the children's movement as much as his owner.

'Curtain twitcher.' That's what dad called her. 'Always listening into people's conversations and trying to keep up-to-date with the latest gossip from the street.' Jack felt a small smile spread across his face as he thought about Henry – what old Mrs Ainslie would give for a piece of scandal like that.

'Psst Jack. Where's Henry?' Codie whispered.

Jack looked over his shoulder. Their mum was still there, watching as the boys approached the bend at the top of the street, where the house eventually dropped out of view. Jack gave his mother one final wave before continuing along the pavement. 'No idea. He must be around here somewhere.'

Both brothers remained silent for a few paces.

The large grassy field to the left of them was bare except for a woman with exceptionally curly brown hair, that they saw most mornings, making her way towards the school. As usual she was carrying her daughter's schoolbag as the wee girl happily skipped her way across the green.

47

The boys stopped at the crossing, waiting for the lollipop man to do his thing, all the time keeping an eye out for their goblin friend.

'Maybe he's changed his mind and decided to go home?' Codie suggested.

Jack shook his head but didn't respond.

The gates to the school were now in sight and there was still no sign of Henry. The boys stopped only meters away from the school entrance.

'Where is he?' Jack asked himself.

'Maybe he's still at our house? He might have got stuck trying to get out of the window?'

Jack shook his head in frustration. 'Can't be, he managed to get in.'

Out of the corner of his eye, Jack, saw Ms Ratch, the deputy head, searching the playground. If she spotted the boys loitering outside the school gates they were toast.

'Psst,' hissed a voice over the cold wind blowing in the children's ears.

'Where did that come from?' Jack said, looking around.

Out of the corner of his eye, Jack spotted Henry standing behind a flourishing evergreen tree at the opposite side of the school entrance. The goblin appeared to be wearing a dark-green dressing gown, with a dangerous number of pockets and which stretched all the way down to the ground.

'Quick,' Jack shouted, ushering his brother towards Henry. No sooner were the boys out of sight then Ms Ratch swung her head in their direction. A second longer and they would have been done for.

'Where were you?' Jack asked angrily, once Codie and he were out of Ms Ratch's earshot.

'I got stuck climbing out of your window, bashed me head and everything.'

'Told you,' said Codie triumphantly.

Jack ignored his brother. 'So how is this going to work? Ms Ratch over there is extremely strict; if we don't appear at school soon she will be right on the phone to our mum.'

The goblin placed a hand on the tree. 'How much time do we have before that happens?'

Jack thought for a moment. 'Must be about quarter to nine. I'd say we've got no longer than thirty minutes before she calls mum.'

Henry looked at his bare wrist once more. 'That should be enough time I reckon.'

'What? Thirty minutes will be enough time to get to your land, return the Tempus Tarda to its owner and get back here?' Codie asked.

'Well thirty minutes of your time yes.'

Jack was confused. 'What do you mean thirty minutes of our time?'

Henry pulled the Tempus Tarda out from his pocket. He briefly turned away from the two brothers and whispered something to the box.

In one swift motion, a small hatch opened at the top of the Tempus Tarda before a delicate looking metallic rod emerged with an even more fragile looking wheel on top. Henry gently placed the Tempus Tarda on the grass. 'Let's join hands so we make a circle.'

The boys were a little unsure, but agreed.

'Are you ready for this?' Henry asked.

The brothers looked at each other before nodding with intrigue.

'Best to close your eyes,' Henry advised. 'I don't want you throwing up all over me.'

The goblin very gently twisted the wheel round clockwise, once, twice and a half. Then he joined hands with the boys and closed his eyes. For a moment nothing happened except for the cool breeze whistling across their faces.

Henry opened an eye first, just to check that it had worked. 'Safe to open your eyes now I reckon.'

Before the children's eyes, everything seemed blurred - fuzzy maybe, quiet, and stagnant. The cold wind had slowed.

'What just happened?' Jack asked looking around.

'We stopped time of course. Well, stopped may be a little strong, but we certainly slowed it down.'

Codie shook his head in disbelief. 'How slow?'

'Slow enough so that none of these other homins can see us or what we're up to.'

Henry checked his wrist once more. 'By my reckoning every minute that passes up here is an hour in my land. That being said, time is of the essence so let's get a move on.'

'Wow wait a minute,' Jack cried. 'So let me get this straight, nobody can see us?'

'Or hear us?' Codie piped up.

Henry clasped his hand to his chunky hips and raised an eyebrow. 'Let me ask you a question, have you never thought you've seen something out of the corner of your eye and by the time you look properly at it, it's gone?'

The boys thought for a moment.

'Judging by your faces the answer is yes. Chances are it would have been a goblin, which is precisely the reason we don't want to be hanging around up here for too long,' Henry said, taking off across the dewy grass in the direction of Harpint forest.

Six

The sun had decided to make a brief appearance, hovering high above before disappearing again behind a batch of angry clouds. The two boys and their goblin friend appeared at the entrance of Harpint Forest. They had only been walking for ten minutes but the weight of their schoolbags was already weighing the children down. The grass around them couldn't have been cut in years and very nearly dwarfed the average height seven-year-old.

'How much longer?' Codie asked, dropping his bag in the thick, wet grass.

Henry didn't break his stride. 'Not tired already are you? It's going to be a long old day for you, my boy.'

Jack's legs were starting to ache too. He'd offered to give Codie a piggyback when they'd been traipsing through the field, but he'd declined.

Five minutes later and Henry came to a standstill up ahead. 'Right, here we are,' he shouted back towards the children.

The goblin moved out of the boys' view to reveal an ancient-looking water well. Growing over the well was a large, oak tree. A tatty wooden bucket attached to a rope was tied round a thick wooden post. Henry looked at the well, clearly delighted with himself.

'I hope you're not expecting us to climb down there?' Jack said, looking down the gaping well into complete darkness.

'I'm afraid so. But not before I've made some safety amendments. We wouldn't want you two hurting yourselves before we even get to my land now, would we?' smiled Henry.

In one swift movement, Henry pulled out a long silver flute from one of his many pockets.

He put it to his lips and began playing the song that he and every other goblin in the Kingdom had learnt when they were little.

Eventually, after a solid minute of playing, Henry removed the flute from his mouth, the faintest hint of a tear in his eye.

'Look,' Henry said, pointing down the well. The boys peered down and to their amazement, the well had begun filling with water. The water filled the well to ground level and then stopped, lapping gently at the walls. It was incredibly clear, a beautiful transparent emerald colour. Neither of the boys had ever seen water that colour before, although once, when Jack had been at the travel agents with his parents, he'd been looking at brochures for holidays to the Caribbean. The water filling the well reminded him of the colour of the Caribbean Sea.

'There is one thing I should probably mention before we leave,' Henry said. 'Remember before I said that you homins had given us goblins a bad name?'

The boys nodded.

'Over the years, Geerah, has spread lies about homins. He's told everyone they are inferior, deceitful and are under no circumstances are they to be trusted.' Henry took a step closer to the boys. 'To begin with, more or less every goblin in the land rejected this horrible nonsense, but, over time, his message is being heard and his support is increasing. Recently he's even started declaring that Trovers and homins are working together – which is nonsense. But if you repeat the same message loud enough, over a long period of time, it soon catches on.'

Henry cleared his throat. 'A new law came into force about a decade ago, which means any goblin with information about what Geerah calls "homin obstruction" is to immediately report it to the crown. Any goblins that are found to have information and have kept it secret will face the full effects of the law. Guilty or not, this law gives Geerah the power to do whatever he wants.'

'What, and everyone in your land is ok with this?' Jack asked, shivering against the cold.

'No, of course we're not.' the Goblin barked, his forehead as wrinkled as a prune. 'We're at our wits' end. Getting the Tempus Tarda back where it belongs is our one and only chance of survival, before Geerah continues his unlawful killing spree.'

Henry ran his hand over his head, before offering a small smile. 'Which is why I'm so glad you two have agreed to help me. Geerah has made some pretty strong technology advances recently and his followers have grown steadily in numbers over the years. He's started displaying false messages about homins throughout the land, utter nonsense – the stuff of a fantasist, but dangerous none the less. Ultimately, he believes that there is some great conspiracy, that Prince James is no longer in our land. That a group of Trovers helped James escape and that he is now living up here with you homins. If he gets one whiff that you two are homins, he won't be forgiving.' Henry said, relaxing his forehead. 'So I will ask you one final time. Are you sure you want to do this?'

The brothers looked at each other. 'We haven't come this far to turn our backs on you now,' Jack said. 'Let's do this.'

'Right you are.' Henry's face was a mixture of pleasure and uncertainty. 'Both of you come and stand up here,' Henry said, hitting the stone base of the well. 'On the count of three, I'll jump, ok?'

'Will we need to take our school bags off?' Codie asked

'Good thinking!' With that, Henry whipped out a small, navy silk bag from yet another one of his pockets. 'Right school bags in here,' Henry said with a smile, waiting for the inevitable.

'Are you trying to be funny?' Jack challenged. 'Our school bags will *never* fit in there!'

Henry's smile grew wider. 'May I?' he said, stretching out his hand.

Before the children's eyes, each of their school bags was forced into the top of the bag. To the brothers' astonishment the bag remained exactly the same size.

Codie rubbed his eyes. 'How is that even possible?'

'This is a burgeoning bag. No matter the contents it never gets any bigger. The ideal present for your mum's Christmas, I'd say.'

The boys were beginning to get the feeling Henry was some kind of goblin magician.

Jack and Codie clambered up onto the stone base and peered down. Codie closed his eyes and took a couple of deep breaths, while Jack looked straight down at the ground. It no longer looked dark and scary, now it was light and clear. From where he stood, Jack, could just about see the ground at the bottom. There were tiny flakes of debris floating around aimlessly in the water.

Henry climbed up onto the wall beside the children. 'This is the plan,' he said matter-of-factly. 'We jump in and swim to the bottom as fast as you can. Pretty obvious really. I will go first and make sure there's nothing obstructing our passage. Count to ten and then follow me. Are you ready?'

The brothers looked at each other. 'As ready as we'll ever be,' Codie replied, holding back the butterflies in his stomach.

Henry plunged into the water with a juggernaut of a splash and began his descent to the bottom of the well. Once he'd arrived at his position he gave the boys the thumbs up, just as they had reached their count of ten.

'Hold your breath,' Jack said, before both brothers plummeted into the water.

No more than ten seconds had passed when a bright light illuminated the entire well.

The boys were no longer in the homins world. For the first time ever, homin children had travelled to The Kingdom of Argon.

Seven

The darkness was obvious immediately. There was no noise, nothing. The air felt warm, clammy, with a noticeable undertone of pickled onions lingering nearby. Codie's body shivered frantically against the damp gloom.

He adjusted his eyes, he could see no sign of Jack, or Henry for that matter. All he could see was water, lots and lots of water. He was completely surrounded by an ocean of liquid darkness. Faint screeches resonated from somewhere up above. It didn't sound like any type of bird Codie had ever heard before. He began to swim, straight ahead, towards the right; it was hard to tell as he splashed away.

Codie heard Jack yelling his name long before he could see him. Then, in-between breaths, he caught sight of his brother standing on a large rock in the distance.

As Codie approached, Jack heaved him up onto the stone and out of the unforgiving sting of the water.

'Are you ok?' Jack asked, worried.

'I'm fine,' Codie panted, coughing and spluttering as he caught his breath. He pulled his now soaked school jumper up over his head and plumped himself down on a hefty gravel boulder. After a few deep breaths, he was able to take in the full extent of his surroundings.

It was a weird, gloomy-looking place. The walls were made of stone, and every time someone spoke or moved a great echo could be heard. It had a hollow feel to it, as if they were underground and from what Codie could see, it seemed as if they were in some kind of enormous cave which appeared to be almost entirely filled with water.

There were hundreds of lanterns hanging from two of the vast walls that bordered the lake on either side. If he scrunched up his eyes, Codie, could just about make out what appeared to be a bridge in the distance. 'You ok there my little friend?' Henry said, making his way across the rock.

'Henry,' Codie beamed, suddenly forgetting how cold he was. 'I'm ok, just glad I got my level five swimming badge in the summer.'

'Wasn't ideal I know, but aqua travel is the safest way to navigate from your land to mine. There were other routes we could have taken but each of them comes with their own set of obstacles.'

'What is this place?' Codie asked.

'Well, I'm glad you asked,' Henry said, pulling out a map from his grubby green dressing-gown pocket and placing it down on the cold uneven ground.

'Believe it or not, we are currently in the middle of Lagoon Lake,' Henry said, as he jabbed a stumpy finger at the map.

'Oh I believe it,' Jack said, taking in his surroundings.

The brothers made their way across to where Henry had parked himself on the ground, huddling together around the slightly ripped piece of yellow parchment.

'Lagoon Link is maybe half a mile from here,' Henry began. 'It will carry us over the Lagoon and in the direction of Periculo. Once we cross the link, we should be safe to gather ourselves briefly before the real fun begins.

'The real fun?' Jack asked.

The goblin nodded. 'From there we have to journey through no-goblins land.'

'No-goblins land? That doesn't sound very friendly,' Codie said, tilting his head to the side in an attempt to unclog the water in his right ear.

'I'd say that's a fair assumption. However, that's not my biggest concern. Remember back in your house I told you how King Geerah had built a wall to separate the Yems from the Trovers? Well that's our next obstacle - The Wall of Segregation. We either need to go over it – impossible. Under it, also impossible. Or through it.'

'Let me guess,' Jack said. 'Impossible?'

'Surprisingly no, but we must time it right,' said Henry. If we can achieve all of this, we will have successfully managed to navigate from southeast where the Trovers live to The Providence, where the Yems call home. From there, we will have a small but precarious journey to make, before we arrive at Periculo, where I hope Naravine will be waiting for us.'

'Periculo. Lagoon Lake. Why do all these places have such silly names?' Codie asked.

'I dunno,' Henry admitted. 'Rest assured, if ever I meet Argon, I'll be sure to ask him.'

'Who's Naravine?' Jack asked.

'Naravine is my friend and the rightful owner of you know what. Depending on how fast we can travel, we may have to find somewhere safe to sleep tonight, before, all going well, arriving at Periculo tomorrow.'

Jack looked around; he wasn't keen on spending the night in this place. It was dark, humid and murky. Large amounts of moss covered the roof, masses of grass sprouting from each and every nook and cranny.

'What's that?' Jack exclaimed, pointing a finger towards the roof of the cave.

'Where?' Henry asked, attempting to follow the boy's finger.

'Up there. Something moved. Something huge!'

'Ah I see it. Don't worry, it's just a bat.'

'A bat, it's massive!

'Nah, I've seen bigger,' Henry assured.

Jack couldn't believe his ears. Sure, it was dark in here but that bat looked about the same size as a fully grown cocker spaniel!

'Don't worry. They won't touch you,' Henry said, catching the look on the boy's face.

'It sure sounds like it's going to be an exciting adventure,' Codie said, not in the slightest concerned about the enormous flying beast up above.

'Exciting probably, but please believe me when I say things could get very dangerous. I know this land better than most so stick with me at all times. If the worst does happen, I will do everything in my power to protect you.'

'Yeah, yeah, yeah. We know! Now let's go and have an adventure!' Jack cried, desperately keen to get out of the creepy cave and away from the mammoth bats.

'Before we set off, I want you to put these on,' Henry said, reaching into his burgeoning bag. He pulled out two dark green cloaks. 'Might be a little on the big side but they will do the job nonetheless.'

The boys accepted their new garments and put them over their heads. Henry then whipped out what appeared to be two Halloween masks and handed them over. Jack glanced at his, then at Codie's identical goblin masks.

'I know,' Henry said, catching the look on Jack's face. 'But trust me, should we come face-to-face with any wrong'uns you'll be thanking me.'

The boys reluctantly put their masks on, Codie trying hard not to see the funny side.

Henry fixed the strap of his bag over his shoulder. 'Right,' he said. 'Ready to make tracks?'

Eight

The brothers and their goblin friend were
making good time despite the emerald cloaks
constantly getting trapped under their feet.
Jack had developed a technique where he
would walk ten paces, pull the cloak up to his
waist, then start the process all over again. He
couldn't help thinking, surely, they didn't
really need to wear these cloaks until they got
out of the cave? Henry however, had been
insistent.

The ground below their feet now felt soft
and unsteady as they walked. Dust stuck to the
children as they broke away from the smooth
surface of the path.

As they continued through the cave, Jack
couldn't help feeling somewhat disappointed.
Since they had arrived here, they had seen the
grand total of zero goblins. Well, that wasn't

strictly true, one if you included Henry, but he didn't count. The more the children got to know him, the more harmless he seemed.

Every few minutes, the three travellers were hit with enormous gusts of wind, making walking in their cloaks even harder. There was also a faint buzzing sound echoing off the clammy walls. The boys could only imagine what this was; perhaps it was another oversized bat simply breathing? Maybe it was a noise from the Wall of Segregation that Henry had told them about? Or possibly, it was the sound of one of these elusive goblins trying to go to the bathroom? The brothers had discussed these theories while they walked and concluded that the latter was the most unlikely outcome. However, as Codie had pointed out, it would certainly explain why they were yet to set eyes on any other goblins.

They had been walking for a good twenty minutes, yet the scenery remained pretty much identical: a big, dark, humid cave. The ever-present Lagoon Lake continued to emit a dark gleaming orange glow every few meters where the reflection of the lanterns guided their route. The clear waters splashing gently against the bordering rocks.

There was one positive as far as Jack could see, those massive bats seemed to have disappeared. He'd been checking up above every few minutes since they'd set off and hadn't seen or heard anything for a good ten minutes. He dabbed at his forehead with his sleeve. It was strange there was sweat pouring from his head yet the cool winds continued to pummel them.

The makeshift path they were taking was made up of a hard, almost-red stone and there were clusters of rocks at the sides of the path all very higgledy-piggledy, from left to right, up and down.

'97, 98, 99 – 100!' Codie said.

'100 what?' Jack asked his brother.

'Rocks. That's how many rocks we've walked past since we arrived here.'

Jack smiled, glad that his little brother was finding a way to keep himself entertained. Numbers were very much Codie's thing. He loved counting, or adding and subtracting – anything that involved numbers. Dad called him a mathematician in the making.

While Jack wasn't bad at maths, his forte was very much spelling and writing. He was top of the class for spelling and his stories had been commended by every teacher he'd ever had - every teacher with the exception of one that is. Ms Ratch, the deputy head, despised children and she'd taken a particular dislike to Jack.

It was known throughout the school by children and teachers alike - not to mention most of the parents, that Ms Ratch loathed children, but for one reason or another, she'd never been sacked from her job. Every day she would usher the children into school, wearing the same grey suit, her matching greasy grey hair in the same bun as the previous day. Her gaunt face, eyeing the children as they tried their best to avoid her. She'd say things like, 'Not you again!' or 'Oh, here comes the stupid one!'

When she was really being mean, she'd come close up to the child's face, close enough so that you could smell the garlic on her breath from last night's tea and whisper: 'Once the belt's back, I'm coming for you!" And she'd really spit the word you. Jack thought back to last week when she'd taken great pleasure in calling him a 'hideous little creature.'

In her early days, Ms Ratch, had been reported numerous times to the head teacher but had always managed to twist things in her favour. Ever since the incident with wee Johnny Smart a few years back, she'd gotten things all her own way.

Poor Johnny had been walking down the corridor, hurrying to get back to class after a toilet break, when he'd seen Ms Ratch approaching. Johnny told his classmates that she'd smiled at him as she approached him, before sticking out a leg and tripping the poor boy up. Needless to say, Johnny had gone straight to the head teacher and told her what happened.

The following day, Ms Ratch had gone to Johnny's class and asked if she could borrow one of the children to help her move some stationery from her office. Unsurprisingly, Johnny was selected for the task. Rumour had it the poor boy ended up in hospital with a broken arm, having "fallen" from a stool while trying to reach some of Ms Ratch's old folders. That was the last time anyone at Lakewood Primary ever saw wee Johnny Smart.

Last year Jack's teacher, Miss Willow, had asked if he would like to stand up in class to share a story he'd written called *The Mysterious Castle*. Things were going great until midway through paragraph three, a knock at the classroom door had sounded and Ms Ratch slithered her way into the room. She had listened intently at the back of the classroom until Jack had finished, and then she had approached him. She'd taken the story from him, sniggering at the front cover that he'd drawn and then threw it down on the nearest desk. Jack had been terrified. Standing up in front of the class had been a big step for him in itself, without Ms Ratch glaring down at him. He could still feel how red his face had become, Ms Ratch hardly needed to say anything, the damage had already been done – not that this stopped her.

She'd bent down, so that Jack was in range of last night's garlic and very softly said: 'Spell Pterion.'

Jack hadn't known what to do. Spell it wrong and he'd be embarrassed in front of the entire class but spell it right and he would have embarrassed her, a life not worth living. He remembered thinking he only had one option.

He'd taken a deep breath, 't-e-r.'

Ms Ratch held up a hand, silencing him, before muttering another of her favourites. 'I'm not angry but I'm sure your parents would be disappointed.' Then she'd simply flicked her head, her way of dismissing him.

Even now, a year later, Jack shuddered when he thought about it.

Henry continued to lead the way through the murky cave, a good ten feet in front of the brothers. As he reached the latest boulder just off the path, he helped himself to a well-deserved seat and waited for the boys to catch up.

'You see that?' Henry said, pointing into the distance.

'I think so,' Jack said, scrunching up his eyes.

'That's where we're heading.'

'Is that where your friend lives?' Codie asked.

'It's certainly in the right direction. How about we keep going for a while longer then we can stop somewhere for a break?'

'That sounds good to me,' Jack said, pulling up his cloak from underneath his feet once more.

The three continued their journey for another half hour. Both Jack and Codie were beginning to feel the pace but were determined to keep going. The farther north they travelled, the louder the buzzing seemed to be getting.

The small light in the distance was growing much larger too. With relief Jack realised it was the mouth of the cave.

Henry pulled off the path and took a seat on the hard, rocky ground. The roof of the cave was much lower than it had been before and could now have only been ten feet above Jack's head.

Henry untied his burgeoning bag and stuck his entire arm deep inside, feeling around for something.

'Ah, here we go,' he declared, as he pulled out two neatly cut sandwiches, wrapped in cellophane. 'One cheese and one ham, so you will have to fight it between yourselves.'

Codie reached out a hand and grabbed the ham sandwich and slightly disappointed, Jack settled for the cheese.

'Thanks!' he said. 'How'd you know to make us sandwiches? I mean, how'd you know we would even agree to come with you?'

'Let's just say I had a hunch. A hunch that you would like lunch,' Henry said, erupting into a fit of laughter that echoed throughout the cave.

The boys looked at each other stone-faced, before turning their attention to their unexpected sandwiches.

'Do you think your friend will be pleased to see us when we arrive at Periculo?' Jack asked, picking at the crust of his sandwich.

'I'm sure he will,' Henry said, as he removed a large flask of juice from his bag.

'Why are you doing it though? I mean won't this Geerah be angry with you once he finds out?'

'Furious, I've no doubt about that. But it's bigger than him. He may be the king but if we goblins don't do what's right, don't follow our path, we'll have nothing to live for anyway. I remember when I was little my father used to sit me on his knee and tell me stories about our world.' Henry said, smiling.

'Stories about when he was young and how different things were. What life was like for him and my uncle, Roggar, before Geerah came into power. You remember when I told you that the species of goblins lived peacefully until Geerah became king?'

The brothers nodded.

'Well, that wasn't strictly true.' Henry let out a small sigh. 'For as long as there have been Kings and Queens in the Kingdom, there have been disputes, coups and attempts to overthrow those in power. My dad and uncle spent their lives protecting King Gola; they even stood by his side at the battle of Mortem.'

'The battle of what?' Codie said, dumbfounded.

'The battle of Mortem – it's the stuff of legends,' Henry said excitedly. 'My dad and uncle, along with twenty other goblins were all that remained between life and death for King Gola. As the army of Timore and his some ten thousand troops closed in, twenty-two of the bravest goblins stood together and battled for their lives, defending King Gola until their dying breath.'

Neither of the brothers had taken a bite of their sandwiches for some time, such was the enthusiastic way Henry recalled the story.

'When the battle was over and the army of Timore had been defeated, ten of the bravest goblins the Kingdom has ever seen were left standing.' A proud grin etched its way across Henry's face. 'The legend grows as time passes. How twenty-two goblins managed to defeat an army of ten thousand, no one will ever know for sure.'

'The odds sure were stacked against them,' Codie agreed, enjoying the talk of numbers.

'I remember once, I asked my father if he thought they got lucky that day, and do you know what he said?'

The boys shook their heads.

Henry put on a gruff voice. 'No son I don't believe that we got lucky. I believe that everything that happens is because Argon allows it to happen. There is no doubt in my mind that he was guiding us that day and when the time comes for you to have your own battles, I have faith in Argon to be looking over you and guiding you too.'

Henry cleared his throat, remembering what his father had said next. 'Despite our lifespan the life of a goblin can be ephemeral. We have rules that we must obey because one day when our time comes, we will all be judged, and it will be Argon himself passing judgement.'

Henry looked down at the ground and then back up at the boys.

'We can only live by the beliefs we have, and I believe what my father told me, despite what anyone else says. At the beginning of time it was the Kobolds who helped Argon in the construction of our Land. And that is why under no circumstances should a goblin ever disrespect a Kobold, let alone kill one. No, old Geerah has made a fatal mistake. Mark my words, his time will come, and I doubt Argon will be very forgiving.'

The trio finished their lunch in silence and set off on their journey once more. Jack helped Codie pull his mask on and smiled when he made a roaring sound - as if goblins roared.

Jack sighed to himself as he watched Codie chase after Henry up ahead. He didn't know if it was Henry's story about armies and kings and battles, but for the first time since they had arrived in the Kingdom of Argon, he felt the slightest hint of regret.

Nine

The cold gusts of wind were blowing faster and faster through the cave without stopping as the trio approached the exit. The buzzing sound had continued to grow significantly louder too. Despite having his gloves on, Jack's fingers were absolutely freezing.

'Wow,' Codie shrieked, getting his first look at Lagoon Link. The bridge looked wonderfully terrifying.

It was connected at either end by a thin, severely frayed rope. Each rope was tied around thick wooden stumps. Horizontal batons of fragile-looking timber were held together by nothing more apparent than fresh air, all of which made up the base of the bridge. Longer lengths of rotten wood connected together over the many gaps on the rancid bridge. And that was only some of it.

About fifty feet in, the bridge disappeared into a cloudy plume of fog.

'I really hope you're not expecting us to cross that?' Jack pleaded.

'I'm afraid so. It's the only way,' Henry said. 'I'll go first; put your minds at ease.'

Jack shook his head. 'I don't know. I reckon if you put one foot on that mouldy bridge the whole thing will crumble.'

The feeling rising in Jack's stomach was hard to ignore. He couldn't help thinking that all three of them had bitten off more than they could chew. 'If something happens to Codie I won't be able to live with myself.'

Henry sighed, resting an arm against one of the brittle stumps. 'Listen to me. I won't let anything bad happen to you or Codie for that matter. I'm indebted to you for coming along with me and as long as we are in possession of the Tempus Tarda, nothing bad will happen to us.'

'How do you know that?' Jack asked. He was beginning to get fed up with Henry's faith in a small, metal box. 'How do you know nothing bad will happen to us? How's that box going to stop us from falling and probably dying if we cross that bridge?'

'It just will, ok? It isn't just some box,' Henry said, standing up straight. 'What lives inside here is extremely powerful and as long as we have it in our possession, I believe it will protect us.'

'We heard you talking to it, you know? Back at our house after we'd had breakfast. Did it answer, tell you everything would be ok?'

'No,' admitted Henry. 'But...'

'But nothing!' Jack said firmly. I'm not prepared to put Codie in that kind of danger simply to return some fancy box to some Kobold I've never even met!'

Jack turned around to usher Codie backwards, but to his horror his brother was nowhere to be seen.

'Codie! Codie! Where are you?' he shouted.

No response.

'Codie!' Jack thundered.

'Over here,' shouted a voice in the distance.

Henry turned and peered over the bridge.

Although Jack couldn't see his brother through the fog, he knew instantly where he was. 'Codie, what on earth are you playing at? How did you get over there? Jack shrieked.

'I walked, silly. It's much safer than it looks,' Codie assured him.

'Don't move. I'm coming across,' Jack shouted, lifting up his emerald cloak and tucking it into his trousers, before marching purposefully towards the bridge.

Henry attempted to barge in front of the boy. 'Please! Let me go first, prove that it's safe!'

But it was too late; Jack was already a third of the way across the bridge, his quivering hands feeling his way and taking him closer to his hidden brother.

Jack's eyes were sealed shut as he repeated Codie's name over and over in his head.

And then it happened. He made the terrible mistake of opening his eyes and looking down as he approached halfway. It was terrifying. He very nearly soiled himself there and then as he stared down at the cosmic drop. His feet were frozen to the precarious platform and he tried to move his legs but they were shaking uncontrollably.

'Keep going,' Henry said encouragingly. 'I'm right behind you.'

Jack forced himself to follow Henry's advice, taking it one rickety step at a time, slowly edging his way closer to his brother. Jack opened his eyes once more. A huge sigh of relief swept over him as he realised he was only a handful of paces from safety.

He took another step closer to Codie, he could sense Henry a couple of paces back. Another step towards safety, his breath sounded so loud, drowning out the sound of the distant buzzing. A couple more steps and he'd be safe...

Without warning, a plank of wood fractured below him. He stumbled and fell forward onto the bridge, staring down at what was at least a 200ft drop; Jack felt a wave of panic. He was more frightened than he'd ever been before in his life. His stomach was doing somersaults and it was taking a great deal of effort not to vomit.

'Don't move!' cried Henry. He loosened his bag down his arm and tossed it next to where Codie was frozen still. The bridge seemed to be lowering, descending millimetres at a time.

A twinge of rope snapping behind him made Jack grasp hold of a rotten section of wood with both sweaty hands, knowing full well it was only seconds before the bridge collapsed.

Henry managed to lift Jack to his knees, easing him up gently.

'Up you get, come on,' he said soothingly 'I've got you.'

Jack meticulously inched the remainder of the way across the bridge, immediately followed by Henry's clumpy strides. As he reached solid ground, Jack crumbled onto his back and let out a huge sigh of relief.

Henry too looked grateful, collapsing in a heap next to Jack. 'Thank Argon. For a minute there I didn't think we were going to make it.'

Ten

Once they'd composed themselves for long enough, the trio decided to continue with their onerous journey. Jack had finally managed to stop his legs from shaking but his hands just wouldn't listen.

As he lifted himself to his feet, something very peculiar dawned on Jack. He had been sitting on grass for at least ten minutes without noticing that it wasn't green. It was purple! Jack pulled a few blades from the ground and let them blow from his open hand.

'Either the bump to the head was worse than I thought, or the grass here is purple,' he said in wonder.

Henry heaved himself to his feet.

'Your head's fine, the grass here *is* purple,' he said.

'But how is that possible?'

'I dunno,' Henry replied casually. 'Something to do with us having two suns, I think.'

'Wow, wait a minute. You have two suns?' Jack said, open mouthed.

Henry looked at the boy as if he'd asked the most obvious question in the world. 'Take a look around. Jeez, maybe that bump on your head *was* worse than I thought.'

The boys looked up at the sky (which thankfully was still blue)

'One....Two!' counted Codie. 'OMG!'

'How is THAT possible?' Jack cried. How had he missed that? One of the suns was the normal size and colour. The other one however, was enormous! At least twice the size of the other sun and it was red!

'Listen, we could sit here all day gossiping about grass and suns or we could actually get moving. We will have plenty of time for chitchat once you know what has been returned.'

'It's just a lot to take in,' Jack said. 'I have only ever seen one sun at a time. Is there anything else different around here we should know about?'

'Probably, you'll just have to wait and see,' Henry said with a smile, as he started trundling off through the thick purple grass.

Jack helped Codie to his feet. What sort of bizarre place was this? Purple grass, enormous gusts of wind, two suns, not to mention the massive flying bats and that strange buzzing sound that was constantly droning on in the background. Jack thought about asking Henry what the buzzing noise was but after the last couple of revelations, he wasn't sure he wanted to know.

Jack and Codie struggled to keep pace with Henry as they continued to make their way north.

Their surroundings seemed to be nothing more than purple grass as far as the eye could see. Great looping hills disappeared off into the horizon. Pale blue skies with a sun strategically placed up above, both to their left and right.

Every so often, the trio were greeted with vast, curious looking, stone structures which poked out of the purple grass, some of which were plain, others had deep indentations, while the latest that they had passed had what appeared to be an ugly-looking monkey with its tongue sticking out, carved into it.

Jack could recall reading a history book at school called *Wonders of the World* which had a few pages about Stonehenge, the prehistoric monument constructed over 5000 years ago. From a distance, the rocks poking out of the deep purple grass reminded him of the pictures of Stonehenge in that book. There must have been north of one hundred of them spread out before them.

As they made their way up the latest knoll, something caught Jack's eye. In the centre of six well-placed structures it looked as if something was... yes, there it was again...movement. He hadn't been sure at first but there was definitely something or someone moving around in the centre of a group of stones up ahead.

'Eh, Henry, what is this place?' Codie asked.

'This is no-goblins land,' Henry said, refusing to break his focus as he answered the boy.

'I was afraid you were going to say that,' Jack admitted.

'But you're a goblin,' Codie said, slightly confused.

'Very true my little friend,' Henry said, still not diverting his eyes from up ahead. 'But I'm hoping if we're quick enough, we may be able to sneak through without drawing any attention to ourselves.'

'You'll probably want to avoid going past there then,' Jack said, pointing to the structure in the distance.

'What makes you say that?' Henry asked.

'I caught something moving a minute ago up there, in the middle of those stones.'

'You what?' wailed Henry, frantically turning towards the boys.

'I saw something moving up ahead,' repeated the boy.

'How very curious. What about you little man,' Henry turned to Codie. 'Can you see it too, up ahead?'

Codie stared for a minute, 'I can't see any....' His voice trailed off. 'Oh, I see it now, up there.' Codie pointed.

'Can't you see it Henry?' Jack asked, slightly confused.

'No. I can't,' Henry said. 'Quite frankly, I'm a little surprised you can. You see, these are Powrie Tombs. Powries are immensely private beings, not to mention extremely aggressive beasts. I have absolutely no doubt that those Powries you can see would have installed all types of charms around their tombs to ensure their privacy, and yet, for some strange reason, you two can see right through them.'

'Is that because we're, as you call us, homins?' Jack asked.

'No, that's even more reason why you shouldn't be able to see through a Powrie's blanket charm. Very curious.' Henry muttered to himself, now certain that he had made the correct decision bringing the boys with him.

Jack looked over his shoulder, although he couldn't see where the purple grass began, he guessed that they must have been at least halfway through No Goblins Land, although admittedly, that was based more on hope than expectation.

Up ahead, the beginning of a very steep hill was gradually coming into view.

Both children's legs were growing heavy again. Each of them secretly hoped that once they had made their way up the hill, they would once again be able to rest.

As Jack took in the full brutality of the hill, he found himself falling behind the others and when he hurried to catch up with them, something made the boy freeze still on the spot.

A hundred feet away a Powrie stood staring directly at him. Although it was skinny, its upper body looked solid, chunky and scarred. A dark brown sheet covered the Powrie from the waist down, while a thick grey moustache sat on top of its lip, the same colour as a patch of hair up above. Its bare feet were fixed firmly to the ground, as its lifeless black eyes pierced directly through the boy. Its razor-sharp yellow teeth grinding together, he was watching, waiting and ready to pounce.

Eleven

Henry had gone on ahead.

'Come on slow coach,' he yelled. But the moment he turned, the goblin realised why the boy had come to a halt. He glowered at the Powrie who was now staring directly at him. For a jittery moment nothing happened except for a murderous staring competition.

After realising that he was walking alone, Codie gingerly stopped and swung round to see what was going on as the Powrie gradually lifted its hand up, revealing a wooden horn.

A thunderous roar blared out of the horn, the sound was one that Henry had only ever heard from a distance, but he knew exactly what it meant.

Without a moment's warning, another Powrie appeared, then another. Within ten seconds there must have been twenty of them, all glaring fiercely at the trio – waiting. A moment later another Powrie appeared out of the largest tomb in the field. This tomb must have been as least twice the size of any of the others, which could also be said for the Powrie which had stepped out of it.

Although a great distance separated them, Jack could tell instantly that this Powrie was in charge. His confident demeanour oozed authority.

The brothers and Henry looked on helplessly as the enormous Powrie let out a huge animalistic roar.

'JACK RUN!' Henry bellowed, scooping Codie up and sprinting as fast as he could.

Jack wasn't far behind, belting as fast as his legs would carry him after Henry and Codie.

For some reason Jack thought he might be safer if he pulled his mask down from his head onto his face but quickly changed his mind, realising it was obstructing his view. But it cost him valuable seconds and when he stole a quick glance behind him fear struck him when he saw how close the army of Powries were.

'They're going to catch us.'

'Keep going,' Henry pleaded. 'We're almost there.'

'Almost where?'

'Up there,' Henry shouted in between strides. 'Once we're over that hill they can't touch us!'

The three of them continued to sprint but every step that they landed the Powries narrowed the gap.

Codie's face was the picture of fear as Henry began his ascent of the purple hill, the poor boy clinging on for dear life as the furious gusts of wind blew harder than ever, while the buzzing sound was almost deafening.

Jack's thighs were burning as he followed Henry up the hill. If Henry was right, they were nearly there. He daren't turn around now. He knew the Powries were gaining ground on them, he could feel it. They were closing in.

As they approached the top of the hill, Jack could see what must have been the exit of No Goblins Land. The purple grass seemed to come to an abrupt end and was replaced by what looked like grey marble.

Towering black fences as high as the eye could see stretched across the marble ground, guarding the secrets that lurked within.

If Henry was true to his word, they were about thirty paces away from safety.

Jack could hear a Powrie wheezing right behind him – 20 paces from safety. They were going to make it. Henry and Codie were a mere handful of paces in front of him. He almost smiled as the excitement of the journey caught up with him – 10 paces from safety.

Jack leapt for safety but was caught in mid-air, grasped by a brawny arm and decisively wrestled to the ground. Henry and Codie had crossed the border to safety, but Jack was in deep deep trouble.

* *

The soaring metallic fences clattered back and forth, as the artificial wind pummelled the trio from each and every direction. The buzzing noise had grown a few additional decibels and was almost certainly coming from behind the towering fences. Each of the two suns were shining proudly in the sky, beaming down on the majestic land below.

The Powrie pulled Jack to his feet with unbelievable ease, before launching him effortlessly down the hill he had just mounted.

'What you doing in our land homin?' the enormous Powrie cried. Several of the other Powries had stopped to catch their breath, although they continued to look on with menace.

Two angry looking Powries approached Jack. The one on the left had a vicious looking scar that stretched from his cheek to below his chin. In one swift movement, he pulled out a razor-sharp spear and pointed it directly at Jack's face - awaiting instruction.

'I was asked to come here by a goblin,' said Jack, glaring high to meet the Powrie's vicious eyes. The boy's hands had instinctively reached for the sky as he took in the full force of the Powrie leader. His long, black hair was straggly and unkept and his thick, hairy arms were like something you would see in a wrestling ring.

'Why?' demanded the leader of Powries.

Before Jack could answer, Henry appeared on the outskirts of his vision.

'Marcel, leave him alone.'

'Look oo it is. Is this your doing? You've got some guts being here yourself, let alone having the audacity to bring homins into MY land!'

Raucous chants of 'kill, kill, kill,' had been started by a few of the Powries.

'Marcel please. You don't understand. Please, let me explain,' Henry pleaded.

Marcel shot Henry a piercing scowl; it was clear there was no love lost between Henry and the leader of the Powries.

'You've got one minute afore I let my friends here run wild and believe me, that won't be a pretty sight.'

Henry cautiously made his way over to Marcel, slowly inching closer to the huge Powrie. A nervous grin crept across the goblin's face, as the two boys and the ravenous army of Powries looked on. Henry stopped millimetres from Marcel as the giant Powrie bent down, edging his huge face closer to Henry. The whisper lasted no longer then ten seconds but whatever Henry said, it worked.

Marcel's expression changed immediately. He looked around at the faces of the army of eager Powries, then turned his attention to Jack, piercing his malicious eyes at the boy, only this time he didn't look angry, he looked sort of grateful.

'Let him up,' he demanded. No one moved. 'Did you hear me? Let him up, NOW!'

Jack got to his feet. Henry nodded at Marcel, before putting an arm around Jack and headed towards the border of No Goblins Land.

'What did you say to him?' Jack asked as they crossed the border of No Goblins Land.

'Just keep walking,' implored Henry.

Twelve

Jack was sore. He'd landed awkwardly on his arm when that great buffoon Marcel had thrown him to the ground. His lower back was pounding, and he had bashed the side of his face on the grass. The boy felt utterly fatigued after having put so much effort in to try and evade the unhinged group of Powries. He massaged his back against a nearby rock in a feeble attempt to reduce the pain he was feeling.

It was dark. Where did the suns go?

In spite of the bumps and bruises he'd endured throughout the day, Jack felt surprisingly upbeat. Maybe it was the adrenalin, but this adventure had made him feel alive, like he was part of something... important.

He didn't have many friends at school. Well, that was being kind. He had one friend and that was only because their mums had been friends since they were kids. Thatcher had been forced upon him from a young age and although he liked him, it wasn't always easy being his friend. Thatcher was the type of kid who oozed geekiness and he had real trouble thinking before speaking, especially in front of Jason McCann's gang.

Yet, being part of this journey, with his brother and Henry, had given him a belief that he was important somehow and that could make a difference. Besides, what else would he have been doing at school, writing stories about adventures and not actually living them?

Codie shuffled closer to his brother, he looked somewhat concerned.

'Are you ok?'

'I'm fine,' replied Jack nonchalantly. 'It will take a lot more than some weirdo Powrie to take out your big brother.'

Henry gave Jack a look that said next time he may not be so lucky.

The mighty fences continued to rattle from side to side. It was colder here, colder, darker and noisier. If Jack's number one hate was the cold, loud noises weren't too far behind. It crossed his mind to ask Henry if there was another route they could have taken, a warm, quiet, safe alternative. As he looked across at Henry's anxious face, though, he thought he would give the goblin the benefit of the doubt.

Jack peered back towards the path they had only just navigated. There must have been two feet of snow bordering the edge of the lofty purple grass, which miraculously ended with a neat contour, melting the snow into submission.

The temperature had dropped a good ten degrees in the space of a minute, not to mention the fact that it was now dark, when minutes ago it had appeared to be daytime.

The route forward was made up of a gravel path flanked by high mesh fences on either side. Razor-sharp lengths of unforgiving barbed wire gleaming angrily around the perimeter of each rumbling fence. As the two brothers followed Henry, Codie pointed out what appeared to be large holes on the opposite side of each the fence.

Jack had been learning about renewable energy at school a few weeks back and he was pretty sure there were giant solar panels above each of the holes.

'So, I have a question,' Jack yelled over the ever-growing buzzing. 'How come it's nice and sunny just there,' he pointed in the direction they'd travelled, 'but it's dark and freezing here? I mean I can still see the sun – sorry both of the suns – shining just over there?'

Henry clasped his hands together. 'You ask a very good question, very observant of you, I must say....'

'So, are you going to tell us, or am I going to have to go back and ask my friend Marcel?' Jack asked, while Codie looked up at the sky.

Henry got to his feet and pointed at the red, larger sun.

'Look at that sun, trust me it won't hurt your eyes. You see directly below it, it's glistening into a sort of diamond shape?'

'I see it,' confirmed the boy.

'You see at the bottom of the diamond, there's a small black ring?'

Jack squinted at the sun.

'Where?'

'I can see it!' Codie beamed.

'Well, that's a molentis key.' Henry folded his arms and confidently nodded his head.

Codie took a deep breath in.

'A molentis key, really? How did you manage to get your hands on one of those? Hey Henry, I have a question,' Codie said, raising his hand as if he was in school. 'What's a molentis key?'

'A molentis key purifies the energy that travels through it and removes contaminates, so we can use the clean energy down here.'

Jack rubbed his eyes. 'I still can't see it!'

'Look harder. Can you see the faint outline of a diamond?'

Jack scrunched up his nose trying his hardest to concentrate. 'Maybe,' he said eventually, as he followed the goblin's outstretched finger.

Each of the boys focused on the sun nearest them, before Codie spoke. 'Are there small drops falling down from it?'

'Yes,' declared the Goblin. 'They are the molentis crystals. Pin back your lugholes because I'm about to enlighten you.'

The boys laughed to each other.

'We goblins have developed an extremely advanced technology, which harnesses the energy generated from both our suns. Those crystals that you can see are being produced through the molentis key. Once the energy travels through the key, it filters down to the ground and is stored in there.' Henry pointed to the fences. 'Inside there are ten Molentis ports, which are basically like big football pitches that stock the crystals. They get processed, mixed together with some materials and essentially act as a power station that fuels our land. During the molentis process, the suns expand to double the size and turn a fiery shade of red. From houses, to cars to bridges, you name it, they are all powered through here.' Henry watched the boys taking it in for a moment. 'Pretty impressive isn't it?'

'Very,' agreed Jack, although he didn't fully understand it.

'These plans were created years ago by King Gola, but have been developed significantly in recent years by Geerah. Easy when you've been handed all the answers. King Gola's vision for this technology was one in which all species of the Kingdom would benefit. Geerah, unfortunately doesn't have the same level of generosity.

'How do you know all this?' Jack asked.

'I know a lot more that meets the eye,' Henry assured the boy. 'There's a small proportion of our land bursting with riches but cross a bridge or two and it doesn't take long before you come across deprived families, who are lucky if they have one meal per day. Geerah commands every aspect of this technology and he uses it to control each and every goblin throughout the land. As I'm sure you can imagine, it's highly lucrative. That's one of the reasons why he hates homins so much. He's terrified that you lot are going turn up and steal our technology and more importantly, his power. You homins are trailing decades behind us.' Henry chuckled. 'You'll get there eventually but it won't be for many, many years.'

'Does the same thing happen with the other sun?' Jack asked moving his arm across the sky.

Henry nodded.

'It does but at different times throughout the day, so we've never got a shortage.

Happened once, a shortage, the entire Kingdom was in darkness for days.'

Jack shook his head in disbelief. It really was impressive. 'Well at least that explains the buzzing sound.' He said, indicating to the molentis ports where ten gigantic metal pumps were hammering away.

'We best get a move on.' Henry said. 'This is by far Geerah's biggest achievement since he became King and as such, it's heavily guarded around the clock.'

Thirteen

'Ah so that must be the famous Wall of Segregation,' Codie said, peeking down from the summit of one of the overhanging cliffs. The colossal wall stretched as far as the eye could see, from left to right.

Jack took a few deep breaths. They really were right in the thick of things just now. They'd managed to navigate their way beyond the heavily guarded molentis ports but from what Jack could see, their ability to be elusive was just about to begin. There were hundreds of guards walking back and forth in front of the wall, on top of the wall, and stationed on various platforms throughout the massive stone partition. Most of the guards were in pairs; some appeared to be carrying pails of water, while over to the left of the wall, other guards were being put through their paces, marching forcefully in different directions. A large number of the guards had what appeared to be small booklets in hand, going through plans or actions for that day.

On top of that, there were various pairs of guards standing at steady platforms cemented into the wall, all of which were looking in the trio's direction through small cylinder telescopes. At a glance, they all seemed frighteningly organised.

'Quick, follow me!' Henry whispered, leading the boys east across the dangerously steep cliffs. 'Stay down! If they detect even the faintest hint of movement, we'll be done for.'

The trio steadily advanced along the fringe of the cliff, taking advantage of the cover provided by a handful of large boulders stationed at either side of them.

They veered right slightly, before a small cave came into view just off-track, while darkness swept over them from up above. The two boys followed Henry as fast as their legs would carry them into the pitch-black cave, unsure what would be waiting for them in the darkness. Jack and Codie rubbed their eyes, trying to focus them, while Henry made his way over to one of the walls and lit some well-placed hanging lanterns, which gave the place a smear of glow. Henry removed his bag and placed it carefully on the ground before disappearing off into a corner of the cave. He appeared a moment later pushing a long thin boulder across the ground, towards the entrance of the cave.

'There!' he said, wiping his hands on his green dressing gown. 'That should keep the cold out! We can rest here for the night. I have supplies in my bag, which will keep us going. We need to come up with a plan of how we're going to navigate our way past The

126

Wall of Segregation, tomorrow morning. As you've seen from that little glimpse, it's heavily guarded.'

The boys took a seat on a large log on the floor. It had been expertly carved and beautifully sanded down, it was so comfy that the children could have been forgiven for thinking they were sitting on their living room sofa. At either side of the log were small, equally smooth mahogany benches.

Henry busied himself collecting some sticks from the corners of the cave and piled them up in the centre of the ground.

Every once in a while, a deafening horn would blare out from somewhere in the distance, shortly followed by angry shouting. Whatever or whoever it was that was guarding the wall, it didn't sound pleasant. With every irate shout that could be heard, Jack was dreading crossing paths with it a little bit more.

And by the look on Codie's face, it wasn't something he was relishing either.

'It's freezing in here,' Jack said, rubbing his arms.

Without warning, Henry, who was sitting across from the children on a stool he'd pulled from his bag, let out an enormous sneeze which conveniently landed on the pile of sticks in the middle of the ground and instantly caught fire.

'Wow that was easy,' Codie chuckled.

'Yip. I knew I was hanging onto that for a reason. I can breathe much better now.'

'Nice,' Jack said, looking around the cave, more in hope than expectation that there may have been a tap for Henry to wash his hands. 'What time is it back home?'

Henry looked at his wrist once again – still no watch. 'By my reckoning, we have been here for just over five hours.'

'Wait, does that mean we have only been gone for five minutes?' Jack asked in astonishment.

'Exactly,' Henry said, with one of his chubby fingers halfway up his right nostril.

'Honestly! I can't believe that after all we've been through, it was only five minutes ago we were standing outside our school hiding from Ms Ratch.'

Codie laughed before agreeing with his brother. 'It does seem much longer than that.'

'That's the magic of Goblins,' Henry said, spreading his hands apart in front of his face.

Henry grabbed his burgeoning bag and pulled out a couple of tatty brown duvets. 'Here, put these on. They're slightly worn but I suspect they'll do just fine.'

The boys gratefully accepted the duvets; Codie swiftly wrapping it over his shoulders.

'Right, what else do we have in here,' Henry said. He pulled out some wet wipes and gave his fingers a good clean before delving back into his bag. The goblin made some strange faces before delving his arm in even deeper.

'Ah-ha here we are.' Henry pulled out a dinner plate, complete with a hefty portion of what appeared to be lasagne and handed it to Jack.

The boy accepted the plate before very nearly dropping it. 'It's roasting hot!' he said placing it down the small bench next to him.

'Course it is,' Henry said, with an almost hurt look. 'I wouldn't go feeding you a cold meal now would I?'

As he handed Codie a slightly smaller plate. Henry then reached into his bag once more and pulled out a couple of knives and forks. 'Bon appetite!' he said, sounding chuffed.

Admittedly, the boys desperately wanted to know how Henry had produced a plate of piping hot lasagne from the manky rucksack that he had been carrying around with him all day, but they both knew Henry well enough by now not to ask.

'Here you go,' said Henry, handing each of the boys a plastic cup. 'It's fizzy juice, that's all I had.' Henry said, unscrewing the lid. 'Don't suppose your dentist will thank me. But then again I suppose it's a celebration.'

'A celebration?' Jack asked, accepting the cup.

'Of course. We've successfully navigated our way through the opening slog. We managed to get here, cross Lagoon Lake and more importantly, managed to manoeuvre our way through No Goblins Land. Not to mention a somewhat heated altercation with the Lord of the Powries. We're doing pretty good, all things considered.'

'All we need to do now is get past the Wall of Segregation,' Codie said optimistically.

'Speaking of which,' Henry pulled a rolled-up piece of paper from his ever-impressive bag and unfurled it on the murky floor, placing a small stone on each of the four corners to keep it flat.

'This is The Wall of Segregation. I'm hoping that before we rest our heads tonight, we will be able to come up with some sort of plan as to how we're going to get past it.'

The boys gazed curiously at the map.

Henry scratched his dumpy chin. 'It's not going to be easy. At any one time there will be a minimum of one hundred guards patrolling the wall, all of which will be dressed, head to toe, in suited armour with weapons up the wazoo. What we need to do, is to think outside the circle.'

'Think outside the box,' corrected Jack.

'That's the spirit,' Henry agreed cheerfully. 'We're not the first folk who have attempted unauthorised entry through the wall. A few years back Frankie the Swindler almost made it, closest anyone's ever come.'

'What happened to him?' Codie asked.

'Let's just say no one's been stupid enough to try it since.'

'Great! So we're the stupid ones?' Jack said.

'Exactly, and that's why the odds have got to be in our favour.'

The brothers looked at Henry with blank faces.

'Don't you see? The guards have become complacent. There's no way anyone would be so foolish as to attempt to cross the wall. Not after poor Frankie – or what's left of him.'

'That doesn't even make sense,' Jack challenged. 'You're going to get us killed.'

'Don't be so melodramatic,' Henry chuckled, 'All we need is a plan. Not just any old plan, it needs to be the best plan ever.'

Jack looked on in disbelief, while Codie, began scratching his head, searching his mind for the best plan ever.

Fourteen

A good twenty minutes had passed in the dimly lit cave; Henry and Codie were sitting crossed legged on the ground next to one of the mahogany benches. Jack was standing with his back to the others, growing tall if nothing else.

Henry blew his nose on his grubby hanky before coughing twice.

'Right, we've done it this time,' he said.' This is it, 100 per cent this is the best plan ever.'

Jack turned to him, frustrated. 'You said that the last time and the time before that.'

'I know I know, but this time it's definite.' Henry rose to his feet. He played a brief rendition of the royal fanfare on an invisible trumpet. 'May I have your attention please? It hasn't been easy. It hasn't been fun. There was a time when I questioned whether we would ever get to this stage, but it gives me great pleasure to announce that we have unquestionably, unequivocally, undoubtedly created the best plan EVER!'

Codie got to his feet and applauded loudly, more to annoy his brother than show his own excitement.

Jack muttered something under his breath.

Henry cleared his throat. 'Here goes. The guards swap shifts at exactly midday and work twelve-hour shifts on the wall. I have looked at it from every angle and without doubt, that is our best chance to make our move.'

Jack exhaled forcefully.

'What, that's it? That's the best plan ever? What happens when they catch us? Because let's face it, they definitely will.'

Henry made a face. 'Don't be so facetious.'

Codie laughed. 'Yeah Jack, don't be so fatecious.'

Jack turned to his brother. 'You can't seriously think that's a good plan?'

'You're right, I don't think it's a good plan....I think it's the best plan EVER! Come on Jack, where's your sense of adventure? Henry's right, these goblins *are* highly trained. It's so crazy it might just work. Let's face it what other options do we have. And besides the Tempus Tarda will keep us safe, right Henry?'

'Right,' agreed the goblin. 'Although a word of warning, these goblins are, as you quite rightly say, highly trained. It is a great achievement to become a guard on The Wall of Segregation. It is reserved for the most elite. It's the pinnacle of a goblin's career and in many cases, a goblin's life! Occasions such as these must be grasped. They're unlikely to give us an opening, but maybe, just maybe if we catch them off guard during shift rotations, we might be able to conjure up a glimmer of an opportunity.'

Jack shook his head, he wasn't buying it. 'So, let me get this straight, the plan is simply to run towards the wall, and hope these elite fighting goblins don't notice us? It would be funny if it wasn't so dangerous.'

'O ye of little faith. Of course that's not the entire plan.' Henry cleared his throat. 'The central gates of the wall are opened once a day. Two goblins from the north are granted access through the wall to the south with supplies of food and drink. I have observed this from afar over several weeks and the lackeys from the north always travel first thing in the morning. They deliver the allocated supplies and make their way back across the wall again shortly after the guards swap shifts.'

Henry let this sink in for a moment before continuing. 'What I'm suggesting is we leave here at exactly 11o'clock tomorrow morning, we overpower the two goblins and with a bit of luck we will be able to slip our way through the wall, posing as the two supply goblins. Simple!' Henry said, matter-of-factly.

Jack gave a firm shake of the head. 'It seems like a pretty weak plan to me.'

'Have you got any better ideas?' Henry asked, somewhat disappointed that the best plan ever hadn't gone down as well as he'd hoped. 'Everyone's great at criticising, you, my auntie Anne, goblins who I thought were my friends.' Henry eyes stared off into the distance. 'It's very easy to talk tough but to stand up against an inequitable monarch, that's hard.'

'What about your mum and dad, couldn't they help you?' Codie asked.

'I don't have a mum and dad,' Henry said. 'They died when I was little.'

A dark cloud of awkward silence filled the cave as the two boys picked away at their lasagne, it was finally cold enough to eat. Although Henry had pulled it from his manky burgeoning bag, the lasagne was exceptional. Like nothing the boys have tasted before, and that was saying something, as their grandma wasn't half bad in the kitchen.

Henry meanwhile had pulled two jars of silverskin picked onions from his mysterious bag. Needless to say they were consumed almost before they were opened. The empty jars were discarded, left to roll off to the corner of the cave.

'Wait a minute,' Jack said, just realising something. 'When we were back at our house, you asked me to get you some pickled onions from downstairs, but judging by the two jars

I've just watched you eat, I'd say you had plenty all along!'

'These are my emergency supply. Normally I wouldn't even think about opening them but I'm low on options, I'll have to restock as soon as possible - down to my last fifty bottles!'

For the first time since they had arrived in the cave, Jack, allowed himself a small chuckle.

He looked over at Codie, who was looking pretty sleepy. Henry must have noticed this too, as he picked up the brown duvet Codie had discarded, before delving into his bag and pulling out two sleeping bags, which he then set up on the cleanest part of the ground.

Codie instinctively climbed onto the sleeping bag nearest him and pulled the brown duvet up around his shoulders.

'God, what I wouldn't give for just five minutes with my iPad,' Jack said, hoping

Henry might have had one stored away in his burgeoning bag.

'iPad? What's an iPad?' Henry queried, as he finished off fluffing up Jack's bed for the night.

Jack gasped. 'Are you serious?'

The goblin nodded.

'How is it possible you don't know what an iPad is?'

'I've really never heard of it. Is it a game, like I-spy? I have played I-spy before, sure is good fun.'

'No, it's nothing like I-spy. An iPad is a handheld technology device. You can play games on it, watch movies, go on social media, almost anything you can do on a computer.'

'Ah I see,' Henry said, sounding as if he didn't see at all. 'Doesn't sound like much fun to me. I think I would rather have a nice game of I-spy.'

'Trust me, if I had my iPad here, I bet you'd be hooked within five minutes. You can play so many games, and there are millions of apps to download at the press of a button - my iPad is my life!' And it was, though his parents had restricted his access recently, something about him not spending enough time outside socialising with other kids. If he was allowed, he would most likely spend every waking minute on his iPad.

Henry sat in silence, clearly not registering much of what Jack had been saying. There was a moment's silence before Henry spoke. 'I-spy with my little eye something beginning with C.'

'You really want to play this game? It's SO boring.'

'Something beginning with C!' repeated Henry.

'Fair enough,' Jack relented, 'Cave?'

Henry chuckled to himself with delight 'Ha! Guess again.'

'I know, Codie!' Jack said, looking over at his brother, who was now sound asleep.

'Hooray you got it!' Henry said, clapping his hands together, causing Codie to stir. 'How did you manage to guess it so quickly?

'Look around, what else can you see that starts with C?'

Henry took in his surroundings for a good minute before concluding that Cave and Codie were the only Cs. 'Right your turn.'

'Do I have to? Jack asked, clearly under enthused. 'It's hardly the most exciting game in the world.'

'Come on, it'll be fun.'

'Fine! I-spy with my little eye something beginning with.....J?'

'J? Hmmm, that's a good one. Something beginning with J. What about Jack?'

'No! Guess again.'

'Hmmm, what about Jacuzzi?'

'Jacuzzi? Can you see a Jacuzzi?'

'No,' Henry admitted, looking slightly discouraged, but it sure is fun to say. Jacuzzi. Jacuzzi. JACUZZI!'

Jack found himself looking down at the ground, feeling somewhat awkward at Henry's outburst.

Henry thought for a couple of minutes. 'You're right this game is boring, let's play something else.'

'No, we've started playing now. We can't quit midway through a game.'

'Well, I don't know, it's too hard!'

'So you give up?' Jack asked, staring to enjoy the boring game.

'Fine!' Henry growled. 'I give up.'

'Jars,' said Jack simply, nodding towards the empty pickled onion jars in the corner of the cave.

'What? That's not fair!' barked Henry. 'Because, number one, that part of the cave is dark you can't even see the jars from here. The game *is* called I-spy. And b, they are Silverskin jars, so technically you should have said something beginning with SJ. And four, you didn't...'

Jack stretched emphatically, fluffed his pillow a little and lay down in his makeshift bed. 'Nobody likes a bad loser you know, Henry.'

The goblin sighed, managing to contain himself.

Five minutes passed in near silence. The only noise that could be heard was the gently sound of Codie snoring.

Another five minutes passed before Henry spoke.

'I know I've said it already but I really do appreciate you and Codie coming on this journey with me. I just hope that all goes to plan tomorrow and you both get home safely.'

Jack rubbed his eyes, sleep was setting in. 'Don't worry about us Henry; we're here because we want to help. I don't know why, but I feel as if helping you is something I'm meant to do, as if it was supposed to happen. Does that seem strange to you?'

'Not as strange as you might think,' Henry said. He wanted to tell Jack now, but he sensed the timing just wasn't right.

Jack yawned loudly and rubbed his eyes again.

Henry caught the bug and yawned himself. 'Get some sleep; we have got a big day ahead of us tomorrow.'

Jack closed his eyes and drifted off into a deep slumber. Henry however remained awake for ages, running through each and every detail of the following day's plan.

Several hours after Jack had drifted off, Henry finally got settled in his own improvised billet. He rested the Tempus Tarda gently on the floor next to him, before doing something he had found himself doing more and more recently. He knelt down on the ground and offered up a prayer to Argon, in the hope that he would watch over Jack and Codie the following day.

Fifteen

The sun rose early in the morning, shortly followed by the second sun. A miniscule glimmer of light flickered through a crack in the cave entrance, just above where Henry had pushed the boulder to the previous night.

Codie was up first, he stretched loudly which woke Jack up, who in turn stretched even more loudly.

'Ah, my back is killing me,' Jack complained, raising his arms aloft once more.

Codie stretched again. 'My back's fine, best sleep I've had in ages!'

'Where's Henry?' Codie asked, looking around their hollow lodgings.

For a moment it seemed as if Henry had disappeared.

Jack scanned the cave, slightly concerned that Henry might have run off during the night.

'There he is!' Codie shouted, pointing to the corner of the cave.

Henry was standing up straight at the far end of the cave, eyes shut, mouth open - sound asleep.

'Henry! Time to get up,' Codie shouted mischievously.

Henry jumped. 'Keep your voices down,' he said, his eyes still closed. 'We're meant to be hiding remember?'

'Sorry,' Codie said, 'but it's time to get up. The best plan ever won't happen without you.'

'I think somebody woke up on the wrong side of the cave,' sneered Jack, winking at his brother.

Henry said nothing, instead he rubbed the grit from his eyes, while scraping the small of his back on a particularly pointy part of the cave.

Jack and Codie were mid-conversation sometime later when Henry approached, looking irritated.

'Time is it?'

Jack looked blankly at Codie, then back to Henry.

'No idea, ever since we got here we've been relying on your wrist to tell us that.'

Henry rolled a sleeve up. 'Oh my, we better get a move on. It's not like me to sleep for so long.'

'You broke into our house and slept for twelve hours straight, in our wardrobe!' Jack argued.

The goblin raised his eyebrows, smiling for the first time that day. 'Not my fault, it was so comfy in there.'

Henry spent the next five minutes what can only be described as grooming himself, while the boys took turns playing I-spy. The revival was on!

'See, not as boring as you thought is it?' Henry grunted, from the opposite end of the cave. He was peering at the boys through a 6ft high, self-standing mirror, unsurprisingly pulled from his bag.

A couple of animated games of I-spy passed before Henry merrily declared that breakfast was served!'

The boys had been so engrossed in their latest game that they hadn't noticed Henry pulling out a couple of plates, complete with scrambled eggs and toast and laying them down on the small wooden benches.

The brothers turned their attention to their eggs and toast while Henry searched his bag for his own breakfast. Unsurprisingly he

whipped out two jars of silverskin pickled
onions and sat down in between the brothers.

After a fierce gulp of pickled onion juice,
followed by an equally fierce burp, Henry's
intrigue got the better of him. 'Any good?'

The two boys remained silent, mouths full
of eggs and toast. He took this as a good sign.

Henry unscrewed the lid of his second jar,
then fished out a single pickled onion before
crunching away on it.

'Breakfast of champions,' he muttered to
himself.

Once breakfast had been devoured, the
boys were each given another cup of fizzy juice
(on the assurance that they once again didn't
tell their parents - or their dentist.)

Once breakfast was finished, Henry threw
all the plates and cups into his bag, mumbling
something to himself about washing them
later. Once he'd cleaned up, he ran through

the plan one final time with the boys. And when they were all satisfied, the three of them decided it was time to continue with their journey.

The goblin removed the makeshift door and set it aside. Both Jack and Codie rubbed frantically at their eyes, attempting to adjust to the glare of not only one sun but two.

The brothers were once more dressed in their emerald cloaks, with the same awful goblin masks from the previous day. Henry had insisted that for their own safety, they once again wore the full costume, even though, as Jack had pointed out, they weren't fooling anyone.

* * *

The trio exited the cave onto crunchy open ground, the fiery sunlight still burning their eyes.

Despite having slept on it, Jack remained far from convinced that their plan was going to work. It simply wasn't realistic. However the fact remained that he had failed to construct a more effective plan himself, so reluctantly, the boy concluded that he had no option but to go with Henry's 'masterplan' – more in hope than expectation.

As far as Jack could see the 'masterplan' was dangerously straightforward. First, they would leave the cave – tick! Then, they would cautiously make their way down the cliffs at the opposite side to the wall, taking things as diligently as they could, while remaining hidden from the guards. They would take cover under one of the many mounds at ground level, where they would wait it out for the two unsuspecting goblins.

If what Henry had said was true, there should be a couple of tired old goblins heading north soon after the trio had concealed themselves. This was where the plan began to take a bit of a sinister turn.

Once the two older goblins were close enough, the trio - well, Henry, would ambush them, taking ownership of their empty crate and lackeys' uniforms, which, in all honesty, seemed a little harsh to the boys.

Once Henry and Jack had changed into the uniforms, Codie would conceal himself inside the crate. Henry and Jack would then haul the crate, with Codie inside, towards The Wall of Segregation and pray that they were granted access.

Having navigated their way down the safest part of the cliffs, the brothers waited nervously at the rendezvous point, while Henry kept an eye out for the unsuspecting goblins.

'Any sign?' Jack asked, biting his nails furiously.

'Nothing yet,' Henry said, looking at his wrist. 'They can't be far away.'

Jack turned to Codie. 'When the goblins get here, Henry and I will go over and talk to them, ask if we can borrow some uniforms. You wait here until you hear me calling you, ok?'

Codie nodded his understanding.

'Aha! Right on schedule!' exclaimed Henry.

Jack and Codie both peeped an eye round the side of the mound. Off in the distance two small figures were approaching, one at the front carrying a wooden crate on sticks, with the other following up the rear.

The trio watched as the two weary goblins waddled across the open ground. Closer and closer they approached the point of no return.

A loud whistling sound echoed out from behind the wall, forcing Codie's hands to his ears.

'That's shift change.' Henry looked at the boys. 'It's now or never!'

With that, Henry fished a hand into his bag and began hauling at something. A smile crept across his face as he revealed a long-handled steel battle-axe.

Jacks expression changed from trepidation to outright fear.

'What are you going to do with that?'

Henry looked at the boys, then at the axe, giving the metal a gentle rub. 'I'm going to do what's necessary.'

Without another word, Henry concealed the axe in his dressing gown and strode purposefully towards the two goblins.

'Stay here,' Jack said, turning towards Codie. 'Remember when you were younger, and you used to lie in bed and see how high you could count?'

'Of course, once I made it all the way to five hundred and sixty-three!' Codie said proudly.

'Well I want you do the same now. Stay here, close your eyes and see if you can count to five hundred and sixty-four. I will go... give Henry a hand getting our uniforms, ok?'

But Codie wasn't listening, his eyes were closed, the counting had already commenced.

Jack bent down and planted a kiss on Codie's forehead. 'Everything will be ok, I promise.'

Sixteen

Jack sprinted round an opening in the mound and set off after Henry, making sure he was still well clear of the firing line.

'Wait up!' the boy shouted, chasing after the goblin.

'Make sure your mask is on properly,' Henry growled, without breaking his stride.

Jack pulled his goblin mask down over his face, as he caught up with Henry.

The two crate-carrying goblins were fast approaching, maybe a football pitch length away. Henry looked different. He wasn't his usual playful self; he looked focused, determined and somewhat cross.

Jack retreated slightly as Henry approached the two grey-haired goblins. The goblin at the front glowered at Henry, while the significantly older goblin at the back of the crate, simply looked grateful for the rest.

'Excuse me, I hate to bother you two gentlegoblins but my friend here and I are lost. We hoped you might be able to give us direct...'

Before Henry could finish his well-rehearsed speech, the angry goblin at the front dropped the crate on the ground and pulled out a much-used bayonet, which had been concealed in his brigandine. Jack stopped dead in his tracks.

'What are you doing here?' spat the knife-wielding, hoary goblin. He had a pale thin face with an exceptionally pointy nose, coupled with a murderous look in each black slit that resembled eyes. Two quiffs of grey hair began at the front of his head and receded south.

In comparison, the goblin at the back's face was far rounder, a plump, almost stone-looking face with a full head of floppy grey hair and enormous black rings underneath each eye.

'We're lost my friend, we're trying to get to Periculo, but we're not sure if we are heading in the right direction.' Henry casually stuck a foot out to wipe away some of the debris from the hard, frosty ground.

'You shouldn't be here; you are in a restricted area. No goblins are allowed here without prior authorisation from the King.'

'Oh, I do apologise,' Henry said, stepping closer to the goblins. 'You see me and my friend here must have taken a wrong turn somewhere down the line.'

In one rapid movement, Henry removed the battle-axe from his jumper and jammed the base of the handle down against the ground. Before either of the older goblins had a chance to react, Henry started chanting in unison with the base of his axe beating the off the ground.

'Boom boom clah, boom boom clah, boom boom clah. Join in!' Henry urged the boy, 'two voices are stronger than one.'

Jack did as he was told.

'Boom boom cla, boom boom cla, boom boom cla,' they chanted together.

Sparks began to fly from the end of Henry's axe, as he continued to batter it off the hard, crisp ground. Jack glanced down at the ground, then back at the two goblins, the crate had now been discarded by both and the goblins eyes were beginning to glaze over. The goblin closest to him seemed to be in a heavy daze. His eyes had changed from thin slits to great round sooty circles.

'One last time, as loud as you can!' Henry bawled. 'BOOM BOOM CLAH, BOOM BOOM CLAH, BOOM BOOM CLAH.'

Henry let his axe fall to the frosty ground.
For a moment nothing happened, and then
the two goblins collapsed in a heap on the
ground.

Jack looked at Henry, bewildered. 'What
did you do to them?'

Henry walked over to the two goblins, lying
motionless on the ground 'We transfixed
them, but we have to move quickly. They
won't be under for very long. Let's get Codie
and get moving.'

Jack ran back over to where he'd left
Codie. His younger brother was standing in
exactly the same position, eyes still closed,
fixated on his counting.

'Codie?' Silence. 'Codie,' Jack said a few
decibels louder and gave his brothers shoulder
a gently nudge.

'Ugh. Jack! I was at five hundred and twenty-six. A few more numbers and I would have broken my all-time record.'

'I'm sorry, but we have to go, now!'

'You could have at least let me finish my counting. It's not easy to keep your concentration for so long, you know? Can I start again?'

'No! We really have to go.'

Codie's face dropped.

'Listen, once we get home tonight we can start from zero, see how high we can get? I reckon we could get all the way to one thousand if we count together.'

Codie allowed himself a brief smile.

'I bet we could get up to two thousand.'

'I'm sure we could but right now we really need to get a move on, ok?'

Codie smiled, 'I bet we can get up to five thousand.'

'I bet you're right,' Jack said with a smile. He gave Codie a hug, the first one he'd given his brother in months. 'Right, let's move.'

By the time the brothers were reunited with Henry, he had already removed the armour from both transfixed goblins and propped them up against the only tree in sight.

Henry had dressed himself in one suit of armour, everything except for the helmet.

'Right put this on,' he said, handing Jack the second goblin's set of armour. 'I've managed to bore a few holes in the crate, so plenty of fresh air can get in.'

With a fair bit of effort, Jack managed to climb into the armour. It was much heavier than anything else he'd ever worn and smelled like a cheese factory. He wondered how long those old goblins had been wearing them for.

Henry opened the lid of the crate.

'Right, in you get me little friend.'

Codie did as he was told, mounting the wooden wall up into the crate. Henry pulled some cushions and a small orange torch from his bag, as well as the copy of Zog he had lifted from the boys' room the previous day. He glanced at Jack sheepishly. 'I knew this would come in handy at some point.'

Codie got as comfortable as possible, turned his torch on and began reading his book. Henry and Jack each took a side of the lid and gently slid it over the crate. Henry picked up the handles at the front, while Jack grabbed the two at the back.

It took the two of them a moment to get their strides together. One of them either walked too fast or too slow. After a couple of minutes, and with a couple of bumps to poor Codie's head, they seemed to get into a rhythm.

And so, the journey towards the Wall of Segregation began.

Every few minutes Jack or Henry would give the crate a gentle tap, just to make sure that Codie was ok.

'Right!' Henry said, after the latest tap. 'We're almost there, so you have to be really quiet now. You need to be silent for the next five minutes. Can you do that, Codie?'

'Sure I can.' Came the response from inside the crate.

'Good! Start from... now.'

The fleet of guards were watching on with menace as the trio approached. Fifty feet away from the gates of the Wall of Segregation and the fear was beginning to rise in the pit of Jack's stomach.

Seventeen

Henry's intuition seemed stronger than ever, as just when Jack needed his assurance the most, he duly delivered. He turned his head round and gave Jack a small smile.

'Don't worry. I won't let any harm come to you or your brother,' he said

A nasty-looking goblin with long dark wavy hair and an unbelievably pointy nose at the centre of his face, sat on a vast ivory throne. He must have been a good six-feet high in the air; goodness knows how he even got up there. His thin haggard face housed a false, uneven hint of a smile, as he glared down towards Henry and Jack. Two broad goblins stood either side of him, wearing repulsed expressions and looking directly ahead.

'Identification?' said the goblin from the throne, his stare piercing a hole directly through Henry.

As gently as he could, Henry lay the front of the crate down and pulled out the small ID card, robbed from one of the goblins he had transfixed.

Jack's arms were beginning to shake with the weight of the crate. He could feel sweat pouring from his forehead.

Henry reached his arm high above his head, still a good two feet shy of the haggard goblin in the chair.

The wavy-haired goblin pressed a small red button on the arm of the chair and, with a swoosh of air, was now millimetres away from Henry's face. Such was the speed that the goblin fell, Jack inadvertently took a deep, very audible intake of breath. Something he deeply regretted as the goblin on the throne now pierced him with a nasty glare, his eyes narrow with thought.

After examining the boy, he turned his attention back to Henry. He reached out a hand and accepted the card, his eyes growing even narrower as he surveyed it.

'Hmm. Give me a moment.' With that, the goblin got up out of his seat and disappeared into a small stone gatehouse. The two heavyset goblins remained completely still, staring directly ahead.

A muffled cough from inside the crate broke the silence. The two stone-faced goblins didn't flinch.

A minute later, the wavy-haired goblin was back. He reached over and handed the card back to Henry. He then nodded his head at a further goblin standing at the opposite side of the entrance.

Instantly, the gates to the Wall of Segregation jumped into life, bumping and banging and slowly creaking open.

Henry put the card back into his pocket and exhaled a cloud of relief, perhaps too forcefully. He nodded his appreciation to the goblin on the throne for granting their access and picked up the crate. He led Jack forward a few feet before coming to a standstill, waiting for the gates to completely open.

Jack arms were now aching, he felt like dropping the crate there and then - but he couldn't, he had to keep going.

He stole a glance over his shoulder. The two wide-set goblins remained static, staring straight ahead. It wasn't them that bothered Jack. It was the nasty looking, wavy-haired goblin perched on the ivory throne. His black, narrow, piercing eyes were fixed solely on him. His dark wavy hair was blowing gently in the wind, while the tip of his tongue poked out from between his lips.

There was no doubt about it. He knew.

Eighteen

Jack forced his head forward as he and
Henry waited for the gates to shuffle open.
The boy looked high up above at a long, stone
gangway that ran the length of the wall. There
were guards everywhere. There must have
been at least fifty, strategically positioned up
above on the gangway. Each one was dressed
in armour, some armed with a bow and
arrows, some with long shiny axes. All of them
with their angry eyes fixed directly on Henry
and Jack.

The gates reached the top of the brace,
banging and clanging the entire way, before
coming to an abrupt halt. The wilderness on
the opposite side of the wall appeared to
consist mainly of concrete. A great open space
of wasteland, that looked as if it housed

174

nothing much except from guards and their necessary supplies.

Henry set off quicker than Jack had been expecting. The boy attempted to grab the handle, but it was no use. The crate slipped through his fingers and battered off the ground. The lid came pummelling off and Codie tumbled out, his copy of Zog still in his hand. Jack froze, Henry turned, looking from the guards to Codie and then back again.

In one swift movement Henry scooped Codie up and shrieked, 'RUN!'

'Stop them!' the guard commanded, springing up from his throne.

Jack sprinted as fast as his little legs would carry him. His heart missed a beat as an arrow sailed past his right ear, no more than inches away.

The three renegades pelted down a steep gravel hill, skidding and bouncing their way

175

down as fast as they could. As Jack landed, his mask came flying off his head and landed helplessly on the ground. Neither Jack nor Henry dared to look behind them.

Codie's eyes were sealed shut as he sat in Henry's grasp,

'Keep going Jack!' ordered Henry.

They continued to stride as fast as they could, well aware that this time if they were caught, it would surely be the end of their journey and possibly their lives.

Henry was now a good ten feet in front of Jack. For being such a wee goblin, when required, he could run exceptionally fast.

Jack kept going, pushing his aching legs into the ground. Villages, buildings and structures were slowing forming in the distance. Oh, how he would be glad when he and Codie were home in their cosy beds, with Dad reading them a story. He could feel tears forming in his eyes. God, even after a day he really missed his mum and dad; what he wouldn't give to hear Sallie screaming her head off at three in the morning. A tear rolled down his cheek and fell to the ground.

He wiped his eyes and continued after Henry, now wasn't the time for tears. He still couldn't bear to steal a look over his shoulder, he didn't have to, he could hear the guards shouting and grunting inches behind him, the gravel underfoot crunching away.

Up ahead, Henry disappeared around a high, fairly precarious looking concrete wall. Ten seconds later, Jack veered around the same wall.

Fear set in when Jack realised that Henry was nowhere to be seen. Then, without warning, the boy was forcefully grabbed and pulled off-track.

It was Henry. He was tucked into the corner, standing in a muddy ditch. Codie was crouched next to him looking extremely worried while Henry was frantically searching his burgeoning bag, scrambling around for something.

'What are you doing? We need to move!' Jack implored.

The walls guards were fast approaching, they were right around the corner. The trio were seconds from being captured.

'Aha!' Henry said, pulling out a long, flimsy metal pole. Although from what Jack could see it looked like more rust than metal.

Henry jammed a finger down on one of the buttons and the pole expanded like an umbrella.

'Stay close,' he said, pressing down the second button. A clear blue shield came powering down concealing the three of them.

No more than five seconds later, the first of the guards came ploughing around the corner and past the hidden trio.

Codie counted fifty-six guards, each of them more terrifying than the last. Finally, once the last guard had passed, the gravel on the ground had settled, all the remained was silence.

The three of them looked at one another in relief. Henry pressed his forefinger to his lips, not entirely convinced that there weren't some straggler guards in their midst.

Finally, the goblin let go of the button and the blue shield evaporated around them. Codie looked up at the others.

'That was a close one.'

'Too close,' agreed Henry.

'What will happen if they can't find us?' Jack asked.

'The land will go into lockdown. If the king realises there are intruders here, he will search every inch of the land until we're apprehended.'

'Why can't we use your shield to get there? And, come to think of it, why haven't we been using it since we arrived here?'

Henry shook his head. 'Can't be done I'm afraid. It will only provide cover for whatever's under it, providing it remains still. If we started moving the shield would shatter, leaving us exposed.'

'How much further is it until we arrive at Periculo?'

'Not far. It shouldn't be more than five minutes.'

'Is that five minutes in our time or five minutes in your time?' Codie asked.

'Five minutes in goblin time.'

'Not far then,' Jack said.

'It's far enough with every single guard in the land searching for us. We best get moving. It won't be long until some of them return to their posts at the wall. We're sitting ducks here. Let's take it one step at a time,' Henry whispered. 'Don't talk unless it's absolutely essential and for goodness sake, stay together'

The trio set off taking no more than a handful of steps at any one time, before falling static and allowing Henry to cover them in his invisible blue shield. Just as they were about to set off again, a horn erupted in the distance. It didn't do much to ease the growing fear in the pit of Henry's stomach.

Another few steps then the same again. The button was pressed and the blue light came shooting down.

Just as they were about to take the next few paces, Jack had to ask: 'Are you sure they're still looking for us? I haven't seen a single guard since they all ran past us.'

Henry turned to look at the boy.

'We're in the outskirts just now, the guards will be in the city. I hate to say it, but I suspect every goblin will have been forced from their houses while they're searched. Once they draw a blank in the city, they'll work their way outwards from there.'

The blue light above their heads began to flicker.

'No!' Henry shouted, pushing his finger down hard on the button.

'What's happening?' the boys asked as one.

Henry hit the button in frustration.
'Battery's dying.'

The light spluttered on and off a couple of times before dying completely.

'Don't suppose you've got a spare in there?' Jack beseeched, indicating at Henry's bag.

Henry scratched his head. 'Unfortunately, not.'

Stepping out from behind one of the mounds, a solitary guard appeared in the distance. His youthful face glared at the trio, then down at the ground.

Nothing happened.

It was as if the young guard was thinking. Waiting for something or someone to tell him what he should do. Just when it looked like he may be sympathetic to the trio's cause, another guard appeared and then another. The second guard reached into his armour pulling out and sounding a thick wooden horn. And then the three guards charged frantically towards the trio, spears in hand, evil intent in their eyes and death on their minds.

Henry turned, in the distance he could see the gates that he'd longed to set eyes on ever since he'd been hidden in the boys' wardrobe. An arched frame above the gates, in golden wavy writing read one word – Periculo.

Nineteen

Henry battered the wooden gates as hard as he could. 'Let us in! We're here to see Navarine! Please, let us in!'

Within seconds, a stony, rugged face appeared at the door hatch. The creature had long pumpkin-coloured hair, droopy long ears and a small button nose. Whatever it was, it certainly wasn't a goblin.

'Please, let us in,' pleaded Henry.

The Kobold stared at Henry and then down at the children.

'What is this in reference to?' he asked calmly.

'We're here to see Navarine, his brother Berke was killed and we have something that belongs to him. But you have to let us in NOW!' Henry screamed.

The Kobold scrunched up his face, as if someone on the other side of the gate had a severe bout of flatulence.

'You will find that I'm the one who decides if you gain entry, not you.' He spat the word *you* at Henry.

The first guard appeared in the distance followed by the other two, each of them bawling something unrecognisable as they approached.

Henry looked back at the Kobold, deciding to fight fire with fire.

'You see those three angry guards? If they catch us, they're going to hurt me and my two little friends here. They'll no doubt steal all of our possessions too, when the time comes, and believe me, the time will come,' Henry moved closer to the hatch in the door, yet his voice grew louder. 'When Navarine finds out that we were here attempting to deliver this,'

He pulled out the Tempus Tarda, 'to him, and you turned us away, you won't have to answer to me, oh no, you will have to answer directly to Navarine. I'm sure that will go down well.'

The Kobold looked flabbergasted. He creased his eyes tightly together and forced the hatch closed.

Jack looked back at the three guards, twenty more seconds and they'd be goners.

'Now what do we do?' He pulled Codie close and protectively stepped in front of him.

Henry didn't answer, instead he remained perfectly still and closed his eyes tight, the Tempus Tarda pulled close to his chest.

A deafening crank sounded as the towering gates briskly swung into life, powering open to reveal the sight that was Periculo. The orange-haired Kobold was standing at the entrance looking on,

'You'd better not make me regret this, goblin!'

'We won't,' Henry assured him, ushering the children through the gate.

The guards behind were piercing through the wind at some speed, teeth bared, eyes menacingly wide.

An almost identical Kobold to the one that Henry had spoken with was standing thirty feet above, on a precarious looking ledge. The Kobold pulled a lever and the gates once more crept into life closing inch by inch and securing the safety of the trio.

The three guards stopped in their tracks; clearly realising that they had no chance of making it. Each of them pulled an arrow from their bag and set it to aim.

'Look out!' Henry shouted, leaping and hauling the children to the ground.

The arrows flew through the air before cannoning into the gate with a thud.

Codie laid his head on Jack's shoulder as Henry got to his feet. He looked around, while a dozen or so Kobolds watched on in some distress. He helped the boys to their feet.

'We made it!' Henry said, sounding amazed. 'I can't believe we made it. We're safe. Those rotten guards can't touch us now.'

Jack dusted down his trousers, while Codie wiped some stew from his face. Henry wore a goofy smile on his face, as if he'd just found a winning lottery ticket in his trouser pocket.

The Kobold which had granted the three of them access approached, still wearing the same anxious look.

'Navarine is waiting for you. Follow me.'

The trio made their way towards what resembled a village, shadowing the Kobold over a makeshift path.

The sky had turned a crimson colour and as the three struggled to keep pace with the anxious Kobold, the orange haired occupants of each cramped, wooden shanty peered out of their doors in astonishment, taking in the features of Henry and his two young aides.

'What's your name?' Codie asked, breaking the silence.

The Kobold glared at the child but said nothing.

Henry intervened, speaking softly enough so that the Kobold up ahead couldn't hear him, 'Kobolds are extremely secretive beasts, just like our Powrie friends. Very mistrustful of strangers, it's wise to wait for them to speak to you.'

As the trio followed the Kobold up the latest hill, Codie reached out and grabbed Henry's arm. A spectacular castle made entirely from blocks of gold appeared in the distance. Jack looked at Henry. He didn't need to ask, he already knew who lived there. Just for a moment he too reached out and gave Henry's hand a small squeeze.

The three of them hurried to catch up with the Kobold. The boys tried to ignore the looks of astonishment from families of Kobolds. They all seemed to have long, wild, orange hair and enough mud on their faces to indicate that washing wasn't considered necessary in Periculo. Their wooden shacks looked in dire need of repair and although they glared quite repulsively at Jack and his brother, the boys couldn't help but feel slightly sorry for them.

Desperate to make a new friend, Codie waited patiently for the Kobold to initiate a conversation, which seemed more and more unlikely as they continued their approach. His thick orange hair slumped over his shoulders, as he bounced along.

The Kobold (name yet unknown) stopped and pointed to an enormous shanty in the distance.

'Navarine is in there. He's expecting you.' And without another word, he turned and waddled off in the direction he'd just come.

Henry turned to watch the Kobold hobbling off into the distance.

'Thanks,' he shouted after him, unsure of what else to say.

The trio turned and looked at the shanty. It was much larger than the others, nicer too, for one thing, it didn't have any holes in the roof. From a distance, Navarine's shanty appeared to be constructed out of corrugated metal, as opposed to rotten wood.

Henry stretched his hands up high in some sort of weird, nervous release. He turned to the brothers. 'Are you ready to do this?'

The brothers looked at each other, and then back at Henry.

'I think so,' Jack said, not entirely sure what to expect. 'But what happens if this Navarine is annoyed at us? What happens if he shouts and gets really angry, or worse, kicks us out of here and leaves us to fend for ourselves with those guards hunting us down? Then what will we do?'

Henry looked at the boy blankly, scratched his head, licked his lips, and placed his hands on his chunky hips.

'That won't happen, you hear?' he said. 'Listen to me, both of you; we have come so far, we've done the hard part. Scaling the Lagoon, making our way through No Goblins Land, we even managed to trick our way past the guards of the Wall of Segregation for crying out loud. Don't worry! From here on in it's going to be a breeze. We're going to return the Tempus Tarda to Navarine, then you boys will be gone from here. You'll be back to school for a day of learning and back to playing on your iPad. You'll be out of harm's way, knowing that what you two brave boys did, helped to save our goblins way of life.'

Henry put one hand on each of the boy's shoulders.

'You should both be very proud of yourselves. If you hadn't agreed to come with me, I would never have made it this far, and the Tempus Tarda would never have made it back to its rightful owner, without you two. I'm sure if your parents knew, they would be very proud of you two.'

The boys smiled.

'So come on, let's finish what we started.'
The goblin playfully rubbed their heads.

The three of them turned to take the final
steps of their journey.

Without a word between them, the trio
froze, fixed to the ground. The only sound
audible was from a murder of crows
screeching widely up above. The renewed
sense of optimism vanished instantly, as
separating them from Navarine's shanty was an
army of at least five hundred guards from the
Wall of Segregation.

Twenty

The two brothers were vigorously thrown into a small wooden cart. A black, metal cage was slammed shut in their faces by a quite revolting-looking guard, before he smiled callously at them through the enclosure.

The boys could just about make out Henry in the distance as he was dragged away, covered in blood and dirt before being slammed into a separate cart.

'Please! Jack despaired.

'What are they going do to us?' Codie said frantically, the fear in the seven-year old's face clear to see. Something that made his equally scared big brother feel instantly guilty.

Jack's foot slid beneath him as he crawled over to his brother.

'Hey hey hey, relax. We have to stay calm if we're going to get out of here.' Jack knew he had to be brave, although on the inside, he felt anything but.

A short, sharp strike of a whip and the horse dragging the cart broke into a gallop. The old cart forcefully creaked into life proceeding over the bumps and creaks of the uneven dirt track.

The cart itself was maybe 6ft long by no more than 3ft high. The floor of the cart was wet and slippery making it difficult to navigate the little room the boys had.

Codie rested his face against the thick metal bars as the last of the snow disappeared behind a heap of purple mounds.

Jack crumpled to the ground, removed his ridiculous emerald cloak and let out a deep sigh of frustration. Things did seem bleak. He had so many questions - where were they going? Was Henry ok? Were they going to get home safely? Were they going to see their parents again? With the last of his energy, he quickly removed this thought from his mind, trying his hardest to hold back a wave of tears he could feel approaching. He swallowed them back and wiped both eyes with his sleeve. Try as he might, he couldn't see a way out of this. He exhaled forcefully once more then wiped the sweat from his brow.

Jack looked across at Codie, who was still peering out of the bars, taking it all in.

A few moments later, Codie, lay down next to his brother. He shuffled around to get as comfortable as the damp surface below would allow, eventually settling on using Jack's right thigh as a makeshift pillow.

Any fight the two of them had left was gone. Any determination the boys had to see this journey through had evaporated too, when they had seen a bloodied and battered Henry being thrown into a cart up ahead. There wasn't much else to do but sit, wait and hope for a miracle.

A good twenty minutes had passed since they had been launched into the cart. The horse pulling the thing was picking up pace, its hooves battering the ground as it galloped away on the desolate surface.

Navarine's shanty had come and gone and Jack couldn't help but think maybe he'd been the one who had tipped off the guards. Then again, the Kobold who'd led them through Periculo could have equally been responsible. What did it matter now? The fact was they had failed and now they'd been captured and were about to face the consequences.

The soft sound of Codie snoring brought a smile to Jack's face. Even with everything that they were facing, his brother could drift into a deep sleep with such ease. It was the same at home, whenever they were being read a story at bedtime, Dad would barely be finished the first page and he could hear Codie snoring away.

Jack looked down at his brother and smiled, then allowed his eyes to close.

The cage of the cart was opened wide by an angry guard, dressed from head to toe in armour.

'OUT!' he demanded.

The boys did as they were told, timidly stepping out of the cart, eyes squinting at the piercing sunlight from one of the balls of gas and plasma high above.

Another guard came up fast behind them, jagged spear in hand.

'Move' he commanded piercing Jack's arm with the tip of his spear.

The boys were led up a steep, muddy hill and then along a winding gravel path, crunching and cracking beneath their feet, still, they had seen no sign of Henry.

The higher they trailed the thinner the air became. Fuzzy clouds of fog were sweeping past them from all angles, while each of the suns now appeared absent. By the time the boys came to the end of the path they could barely see two feet in front of them.

'Don't stop. Keep moving until *I* tell you to stop!' spat the guard. Jack put his arm around Codie as they continued to take small steps forward, each of them utterly terrified about what was to come.

Jack's hands were shaking and he could feel sweat pouring from his forehead as he inhaled a deep breath of the cool, clammy air.

Codie reached out and grabbed his brother's arm as a towering structure came into view. The closer he got, the more spectacular the golden castle seemed. Jack looked up at the purple flags that were sticking out of each turret, all of them had a black Y in the middle. The guard jabbed the blunt end of his spear into Jack's back, forcing the youngster forward.

The children made their way through the open portcullis and across the extensive courtyard, six guards stationed at the entrance to the castle came into view, each one stood no more than a foot away from the other.

As the boys approached, the two guards in the centre stepped aside to grant the children access.

Once they were inside, the spear wielding guard continued to bark instructions as he led the boys through a vast hall.

'Come on, hurry up! Turn left! Turn Right! Keep walking!' And, what appeared to be his favourite. 'Just you wait!'

In a strange kind of way, the guard reminded Jack of Ms Ratch.

If outside of the castle was spectacular, the inside was nothing short of decrepit. It was dull and murky and smelled horrible, like damp towels mixed with yesterday's socks. The walls were painted from top to bottom in dark red, finished off with a bold, golden border halfway up. The gravel below their feet had been replaced with a threadbare brown carpet. It was as if whoever built the castle, had spent their entire budget on the outside structure and completely neglected the fact that they also had to furnish the inside.

Glowing lanterns were fixed from cracked walls on either side giving the place enough of a glow to see only the next step ahead. Droplets of water were falling often and heavy from the ceiling, as the boys, under duress, continued to walk. The tip of the guards spear only inches away.

Eventually they came to a set of varnished mahogany double doors, which opened from the inside to reveal a bewildering sight.

A great, opulent circular auditorium full entirely, from front to back and top to bottom of goblins. There were no lanterns in here, Jack scrunched up his eyes as he looked at the distant ceiling, where five marvellous chandeliers were hanging, each one complimented with a dozen lit candles. There were lavish portraits of ugly goblins, some of which were smiling; the majority though looked very displeased.

Silence plagued the room as the children were ushered along the walkway. Some of the goblins turned their disapproving attention to the boys as the mahogany doors behind them were locked. Most of the crowd, however, had their eyes fixated on whatever was happening up ahead.

The brothers were forced down the walkway towards the centre of the room by the pushy goblin, who had decided to rest his spear aside when the doors had closed. The silence was occasionally drowned out by members of the crowd who had decided to stand and shout muffled obscenities at the boys.

Jack gasped as Henry came into view. He was on his knees in the centre of the floor. His hands bound behind his back. His face was covered in dried blood and his bottom lip was swollen. Visible clusters of tears had formed at the corners of his eyes.

Codie ran over to the goblin. 'Are you ok?' he said, pulling Henry into a warm embrace.

Jack was thrown down to the floor beside the others. An outpouring of laughter erupted in the auditorium at Codie's affection for the goblin.

Henry looked at the two boys and sniffed.

'I'm all right. I just wish I hadn't gotten you two involved in this mess.'

Jack reached over and grabbed Henry's shoulder, 'Don't worry. We're with you to the end, no matter what.'

Twenty-one

The auditorium fell deadly quiet as a salient goblin dressed in a large purple surcoat appeared through a wooden door at the back of the auditorium. The goblin had a worn, hardened face with a trim white beard. A radiant crown sat on top of shoulder-length thick white hair. He had an extensive scar in the shape of a half-moon, which curved dangerously close to his right eye.

'No prizes for guessing who that is,' uttered Henry.

King Geerah made his way up towards the podium and took a seat on his immense throne. His eyes were sunk almost inconceivably deep into his head. His small, thin lips sat below an uncomfortable pointy nose, which from the boys' viewpoint contained about as much white hair as his head.

A stout, tired looking goblin walked over to the king and placed a manila folder down on his podium.

The king pulled a pair of half-moon glasses from the breast pocket of his purple surcoat, opened the folder and removed a piece of parchment. The room waited, as the king's eyes skimmed from left to right.

After a moment, Geerah removed his glasses and placed them back in to his pocket. He stood up from his throne before addressing the room, intentionally ignoring the trio directly in front of him.

'In light of recent events, we must all pay a tremendous debt of gratitude to the brave guards of the Wall of Segregation. These courageous goblins risk their lives each and every day to ensure our safety remains intact.'

The king cleared his throat. 'Admittedly, this is the first security breach we have suffered for many years, but it highlights the need for each and every goblin to remain vigilant against the treacherous forces who aim to undermine our way of life.'

The crowded auditorium listened intently as their monarch continued his proclamation.

'Regardless of age, gender or race, I have always tried my best to protect the occupants of our land from evils that wish to do us harm.'

Henry shook his head in disbelief. He couldn't believe the lies that were coming out of Geerah's mouth.

The King lowered his head, assessing the three figures in the centre of the room, his attention fixated on Henry. 'Taking homins into our world is not only morally questionable, it is, as you are well aware, illegal. The rules exist for a reason and must be followed. This is not only to protect our deeply sought-after resources, but to protect each and every one of you. Let us not forget, that for the next five decades, at least, our children, grandchildren and generations beyond, will be able to live in a world at the forefront of science, due to the advances in technology made throughout MY reign. This has made us the envy of the homin species, which is precisely the reason why mingling with them is not only strongly discouraged - it is forbidden!'

Henry could sit in silence no longer.

'But these homins are not bad. They only came here because I asked them to.'

'SILENCE!' The king demanded, standing up from his throne. 'Not only was your quest foolish, it was completely unachievable. To think that a worthless, futile goblin such as yourself and these two young homins, would be capable of coming here, and outsmarting MY elite guards was downright foolish!'

King Geerah stroked his thin white beard for a moment.

'Many years ago, there was a young goblin that grew greedy with power. He craved the spotlight in such a way that he would have brought much death and suffering to our kind. This egotistical, self-centred goblin even killed his own father, my brother, in his own selfish interests.'

'That's a lie.' Henry roared, a layer of spite in his voice.

The king continued, seemingly unfazed. 'It is for this reason that the punishment must be harsh and it must be immediate. There can be no delay with a crime this serious.'

Geerah studied the crowd of goblins that filled the congested room. Lingering on some, keen to see how long his devotees dared to look into his eyes. Finally, the king turned his attention back down to the three prisoners on the floor. Geerah clicked his fingers and two guards pounced on Henry, hauling him to his feet.

'Search him., the king commanded.

The two guards did as instructed, being as rough as they liked. Jack and Codie looked on helplessly.

With a gloved hand, one the guards pulled something out of Henry's pocket.

'Found it my lord.'

The guard handed the Tempus Tarda over to King Geerah, before throwing Henry back to the ground. His burgeoning bag came loose and landed on the floor next to him.

King Geerah smiled at the Tempus Tarda.

'I believe this belongs to me. It looks as if we will have to add theft to the ever-growing list of offences you have committed in the last 24 hours.'

'You stole if first,' Henry said, defiantly fighting back the tears. That belonged to Berke, the Kobold, and you stole it from him!' The auditorium erupted into a fit of laughter. The king even allowed himself a wild cackle.

Henry forced himself to his feet; he could no longer suppress the wave of anger he felt. 'You stole it from him, and then you killed him!'

King Geerah raised a hand, the crowd fell silent instantly. The smile had gone, replaced with a fierce penetrating glare of contempt.

'You will spend the night in the dungeons,' the king declared, glaring out into the crowd, then back at Henry. 'For the crimes that have been brought against you, it's imperative that you suffer the most severe of punishments.'

The king composed himself for a moment before turning his attention back to the wounded goblin on the floor. 'As such, you will be put to darkness at first sunrise tomorrow morning.' The king banged his gavel down on the podium and the crowd of goblins erupted into hysteria.

As the king got up to leave, a loud banging sounded on the doors of the auditorium. An uneasy hush fell over the room, so much so that even King Geerah looked slightly concerned. Another emphatic bang and the towering mahogany doors were battered open.

You could hear a pin drop as a hooded figure approached the centre of the auditorium. Slowly the figure made its way up the isle towards the King Geerah.

'Who goes there?' the king asked in a trembling voice.

The figure kept on walking, hood low as it went.

The king got to his feet, slammed a hand on his podium.

'Who goes there?' he demanded.

The hooded figure stopped as it reached the centre of the auditorium. Eight of the closest guards had their weapons directly fixed on the figure, but none dared attack until they were given the order.

The figure slowly reached up and pulled down its hood.

Jack and Codie looked on in a stunned silence as their father looked down at them.

Twenty-two

Jack and Codie instinctively leapt up from the ground and threw their arms around their dad. The consequences of their actions no longer seemed as great a concern, now that their father was here to protect them.

The entire auditorium was deadly quiet for at least a minute, not even King Geerah could articulate a suitable response.

After what seemed like an eternity Jack opened his eyes. A small part of him had completely forgotten where they were and the fact that there were hundreds of angry goblins one command away from pouncing on them.

'Wait a minute,' Jack said, pushing his face away from his dad. 'We used the Tempus Tarda to slow down time outside our school; the only way you could be here is, if you weren't affected by us slowing down time.' His eyes widened. 'And the only way that that would be possible is...is... if you're a goblin!'

The boy's father smiled at them. 'I guess you discovered my secret!'

Henry turned to the boys, his poor face a mixture of bruises and blood.

'It wasn't by chance that I arrived at your house yesterday and fell asleep in your wardrobe,' he said. 'There was a reason for it. A reason I now know to be true.' The goblin smiled at James.

An elderly goblin, with grey, shoulder-length hair, placed a withered hand on the railing ahead of him and heaved himself up, rising to his feet in the middle row of the auditorium. The goblin ever so slowly raised his hand and pointed his shaky, index finger at the children's father. When he spoke it was soft, gentle and raspy.

'It's the lost prince,' he said. 'The lost prince has returned.'

King's Geerah was aghast. He hadn't moved or spoken since James had revealed himself. An eerie silence broke out across the stunned room. The realisation that after seventeen years, Prince James, had finally returned to the Kingdom had, it seemed, left the room bewildered.

Ever since James had disappeared, goblins throughout the land were convinced he was dead, killed by the sword of Geerah. The longer the prince had remained missing, the larger and more elaborate the rumours became. Goblins to the east truly believed that an enormous battle that lasted three weeks straight, had taken place in The Providence. Thousands of goblins had perished, which in the end, resulted in a final encounter between Prince James and the future King Geerah.

There were many pockets of goblins that, despite his absence, had remained faithful to the old king and the lost prince. Some of them had even spent years searching for him in secret, convincing each other that Prince James was still alive and reassuring anyone that would listen, that he would one day return. Well today was that day.

King Geerah's pale face looked horrified. He climbed unsteadily to his feet. 'This is not a reunion of some old friend,' He spat, jabbing a long pointy finger at James. 'This goblin is responsible for the death of your king, my brother and his own father. If he is prepared to go to such sinister lengths to be ruler of this land, he is not to be welcomed back into our midst like some lost hero. No. He is to be held accountable for his crimes.'

Geerah turned to look directly at James, allowing himself a deep breath before he said, with genuine interest: 'I must say you do look different, your ears and face have clearly undergone some kind of transformation. Tell me, how did you manage to fool those homins into thinking you were one of them?'

'Once the ears are clipped, you'd be surprised how quickly our kind can look like a homin. All you really need is some makeup, a couple of prosthetic legs and some homin clothes,' James said.

'Prosthetic legs you say. I would never have guessed.'

The eight guards remained fixed on James, spears in hand, waiting for their King to give the command.

Geerah was clearly beginning to grow in confidence, the colour flooding back to his cheeks.

'Well, I do not doubt that we could sit here and reminisce all day; however, you are unfortunately interrupting an ongoing hearing.' Geerah clicked his finger. 'My guards will escort you to the dungeons until such time as a suitable punishment for your crimes can be determined.'

'What crimes?' Questioned James, looking distastefully towards Geerah.

King Geerah shot James a piercing look. 'You killed the king and must be held accountable.'

'That's a lie,' Henry shouted.

'I beg your pardon?' spat Geerah. 'I would encourage you to remember where you are and who you are addressing you filthy little heathen!'

Henry got to his feet, his face continued to bleed, and his hands remained bound behind his back. 'You killed King Gola, not James, and I can prove it!'

The king said nothing, while the colour once more sapped from his face.

Henry whispered something entirely undetectable to the room full of goblins.

With a tremendous burst of energy, the Tempus Tarda flew from Geerah's grasp, crashing along the ground before coming to a stop at Henry's feet.

The king grunted, 'What's going on here? What lies have you constructed?' He raised a hand and a row of guards tightened their grip on their spears.

Henry bent down and whispered something to the Tempus Tarda then turned his attention to King Geerah.

'You thought you got away with it but you didn't, someone saw you that night, saw exactly what you did.' Henry nonchalantly looked down at the Tempus Tarda and nodded. At once, a black plume of smoke began funnelling out of the Tempus Tarda and filled the room, projecting high above towards the ceiling.

It was difficult to tell as the cloud of smoke was thick and black, but it appeared to be forming a grainy bird's eye view of the Kingdom. The smoke jumped, spluttered and wheezed, before forming, what was now recognisable as Geerah's castle. If the sight above the crowd was grainy at first, it was now crystal clear for all to see.

The thick smoke manipulated itself, backwards, forwards, in a circle, before pulling itself together to reveal a strapping, confident goblin, dressed in silk robes, with a crown upon his head. The goblin was smiling as he strode forwards and sat down opposite a younger goblin, dressed in orange robes. The two goblins appeared to be playing some sort of board game, great smiles plastered on each of their faces. Although there was no sound, it was clear to all who watched it, that the two smoky protagonists had a great affection for one another.

Geerah's guards continued to wait for a sign, but their king was frozen stiff.

The crowd looked on in trepidation as the footage sprang back into life showing the same confident goblin in his chambers. He was sitting on the edge of a bed, his mouth moving back and forth. The young goblin was now lying down in the bed sound asleep. The only movement in the chamber was a candle that sat flickering away on the windowsill. The smoke enveloped once again as a door appeared at the far end of the room. A crass, bony goblin stood looking on. His face was a picture of hatred and despair. His hollow features were youthful, but there was no mistaking that it was King Geerah who stood in the doorway.

In the centre of the room, Geerah crumbled to his seat but opted not to speak. Still his guards waited for the order.

The smoke footage combined for a third and final time. This time, the confident goblin no longer appeared happy, instead, he was visibly anxious, pacing back and forth in his chambers. His crown was placed on the table next to him as he made his way over to the door.

The bony face of a youthful Geerah appeared at the entrance of the chamber. A muted conversation took place, followed by the anxious goblin collapsing to the ground in a heap. Geerah put a hand on the goblin's shoulder, but his false attempt at reassurance did no good. The goblin was inconsolable, broken on the floor. The smoke showed

Geerah making his way over to a small cellaret in the corner of the room, before taking out two glasses and filling them with liquor.

The smoke puffed and sizzled and turned a shade of maroon as Geerah walked past the broken goblin on the floor.

Geerah then removed a small flask from his pocket, tipping three drops of liquid into one of the glasses, before casually dropping the flask back in his pocket.

Geerah spun round and, using all the effort he possessed, he helped the distraught goblin to his feet. A tense conversation took place then Geerah handed the contaminated glass to his brother.

The smoke lingered just long enough in the sky to show King Gola taking a long gulp of the glass. Within seconds, he dropped the glass to the ground and began frantically grabbing at his throat. No more than thirty seconds had passed since King Gola put the glass to his lips and there he lay, sprawled out on the ground, choking, spluttering and gasping for breath, before finally falling still, flat on his back.

The dusty clouds of smoke particles fell slowly towards the ground, gently floating back into the Tempus Tarda, which had remained at Henry's feet.

Throughout the auditorium, audible gasps of shock had been noticeable during the entire smoke show, but none as apparent as the last one.

James looked up at Geerah.

'That was the day I went missing wasn't it?'

Geerah said nothing.

'After months and months of asking, that was the day you told me we could finally go hunting, wasn't it? Just as long as it was our secret. You told me not to tell my father because you didn't want him to worry. I can remember how excited I was.,' James said, looking furiously at his uncle. 'But when we got there, into the deepest part of the woods, you threw me to the ground, told me that my father didn't love me anymore and that he'd asked you to take me out here to get rid of me.'

Both Jack and Codie were terrified, they had never seen their father cry before but just for a moment it looked as if it might happen.

James's sorrow quickly turned to anger. 'Is that why he was pacing back and forth, because he didn't know where I was? He thought I was dead?'

Geerah again said nothing. His head bowed down towards the ground, like a child who had been caught helping himself to a sweet before supper.

James turned his back on the king and addressed the auditorium.

'Is this really the type of king you want presiding over you? A king who is so driven by power, he will pretend his nephew is dead, and then when our true king, his brother, was at his most vulnerable, this despicable parasite poisoned him in cold blood.'

The crowd of goblins began shaking their heads, some even shouted out in anger at the disgraced king.

Sensing that this may be one and only opportunity to regain dominance, King Geerah threw himself up from his chair and lunged at James. He may have been over 150 years old, but he was still quick on his feet.

Geerah's guards were a little slow to react, surprised by the sheer speed of their king. It didn't take them long however, to react, standing to attention with their spears at the ready. Unfortunately for Geerah, he was lunging at someone who much younger, quicker and determined to avenge his father.

James managed to sidestep the lunging king, leaving Geerah to fall, angrily, to the ground in a crumpled heap.

The crowd of goblins rose to their feet in unison, some shocked, some angry, each and every one of them with their own allegiance. Volcanic outbursts of encouragement from half the room, slurs of abuse from the other half.

A rough circle formed in the centre of the room by some of the crowd, who were far too animated to remain in their seats. Some of Geerah's guards found themselves in angry confrontations with members of the crowd, while others were shouting and brawling with each other. Most of the crowd, however, had their eyes fixed on the centre of the circle, where Geerah and James stood alone.

The last thing either of the brothers saw before Henry scooped them up, was the anger on their father's face - anger that neither brother had ever been unfortunate enough to experience before.

'Get off of me!' Jack demanded. 'I need to help my dad.'

'Let us go!' Codie shouted.

The boys couldn't believe how strong Henry was. They wriggled and pushed and struggled but it was no use, Henry wasn't letting go.

'Stop it!' Henry screeched, over the sound of the ferocious crowd. 'Your father doesn't need your help. He needs to know you're safe.'

The goblin pushed his way through a metal door and slammed it shut with his foot, whispering something as he went. The shouting and screaming coming from the angry crowd was instantly muffled.

'Stay here,' Henry pleaded, dropping the boys down in the corner of a small, empty room.

Both brothers threw themselves at the door and started frantically pulling at the handle.

'It's no use,' Henry said in a sombre voice. 'Try it as much as you like. I've bewitched the door, it won't budge.'

Jack wasn't giving up. He pushed, pulled and even kicked the door to no avail. The thick, steel door held firm. He could have hit the thing for hours and he'd doubt it would even make a dent.

The boy turned furiously to Henry.

'Why would you do that? My dad came here to save us and you've left him out there by himself. Geerah and his guards will kill him!'

Codie sat down teary-eyed in the corner and put his head in his hands. It was all becoming too much for the young boy to process.

'Do you really think I would let that happen?' Henry cried.

'How are you going to stop it when you're trapped in here with us?'

Henry pulled out the Tempus Tarda and held it out; he'd only just managed to grab it before to scooped the boys up. 'This is how I know. If we trust the Tempus Tarda.'

Jack had heard enough, he thumped the Tempus Tarda out of Henry's hand, watching as it clattered off the stone wall.

'Shut up about that stupid thing! You keep going on about it as if it's magic or something. Let's face it; it's an ugly silver box - that's it! It's not going to keep us safe or change the future and if you think that it is, then you're deluding yourself!'

The shouting and banging continued on the outside of the room, while Jack trundled over and sat on the stone floor, beside his brother. It was hopeless. Anything could be happening to his dad and thanks to *Henry,* he was powerless to stop it.

Henry dejectedly made his way over to the Tempus Tarda at the opposite end of the room. He picked it up and gently cushioned it in both his hands. Then he fell to the ground cradling the Tempus Tarda, hoping and praying that Argon's divination had been right.

Twenty-three

The ground had stopped shaking, outside the room, the muffled shouting of the crowds had concluded, and the brawling had, it seemed, ended. The air in the locked room had become stuffy and stale. All that remained was silence. Silence and hope.

Jack pulled himself to his feet, wiped the back of his arm across his forehead. Small particles of dust were floating up ahead of him. There was a narrow gap between to door and the wall which allowed a smidgen of sunlight to shine through.

'How long have we been in here?' Codie asked, wiping his eyes.

'Too long!' Jack growled, glaring at Henry.

The goblin got to his feet.

'I'm sorry, ok? Maybe I shouldn't have locked us in here, but I panicked, I didn't know what else to do.'

'Maybe you should have let us decide, instead of picking us up and dumping us in this horrible room against our will!'

Henry said nothing for a moment and then let out a deep sigh.

'You're right. For too long I have been living my life looking for answers when they don't exist. When what I really should have been doing is simply living. Ever since my parents died, I've forced myself to look for answers. A justification for everything that happens, good or bad, instead of accepting it. I put my faith in the Tempus Tarda.' A solitary tear trickled down Henry's right cheek. 'I'm sorry I locked us in here. I just did what I thought was best, what I thought would keep you two safe.' Henry cleared his throat. The tears were streaming down each of his cheeks now.

The brothers glanced at each other, then across to where Henry stood in the centre of the room. Jack could feel an uncomfortable strain of guilt tugging at his salivary gland, rising through his stomach up towards his mouth, finishing in his own teary eyes. He leapt over to Henry and pulled him into a warm embrace.

'I'm sorry too,' Jack said.

Codie heaved himself up off the cold ground, made his way across the room and grabbed hold of each of them around their stomachs.

For just a moment all was quiet.

Jack pulled his head away from Henry.

'We need to find out what's going on out there.'

'But how are we going to get out?' Codie asked. 'The door's sealed shut.'

'Maybe we don't have to get out,' Jack said, spying a small vent directly above the door. 'Quick, both of you give me a hifty up to that window.'

Henry and Codie followed Jack over to the door; none of them had the first clue of what a hifty may be.

Sensing this, Jack intervened. 'Connect your hands together then let your fingers slip through.'

Codie and Henry did as they were told.

'Right, now put your hands down,' Jack instructed. He put his right hand on the door, before lifting up his left leg and placing it on the small platform Henry's hands had created.

Jack edged his way up the door, slowly pulling his head in line with the vent. He stretched his neck as far as it would go in order to steal a glimpse at the outside world. He was edging closer, only millimetres away when, with an almighty force, the door was hauled open. Jack lost his footing and tumbled awkwardly to the ground.

'DAD!' Codie shouted, climbing over his brother and latching onto James.

'Hey buddy, James said. 'Oh, I'm so glad to see you two!'

Henry helped Jack back to his feet, before Jack too, threw himself towards his father, burrowing his face in his dad's shoulder.

Jack couldn't contain the euphoria he felt at seeing his father safe and well again. He couldn't care how many people were watching from the auditorium. All he could think about was how happy he was to be reunited with his father.

After a long moment, Jack and Codie pulled their faces away, each of them leaving a wet mark on his father's shirt.

'Where's King Geerah?' Jack asked.

His father looked down at son and smiled.

'Always worrying. Forget about him, he's gone.'

'Is he gone for good?' Codie asked, still clinging around his father's waist.

His father sighed and looked up at the sky, 'I certainly hope so.'

* *

'Difficult and precarious times lie ahead,' said James, addressing the now semi-full auditorium. 'On this day, I stand here because King Geerah has been defeated.'

The crowd of goblins that remained in the auditorium burst into applause.

240

'However,' James continued. 'I do not believe for one minute that this will be the end of our challenges. There will always be goblins with new plans and ideologies that wish to do us harm, to threaten our way of life and to create suffering throughout our great Kingdom. It is for these reasons that this land must have a strong and courageous leader. It must be someone who each of you can trust and depend on during the challenging times that lay ahead. It's essential that this goblin have a great deal of integrity, not only to deal with the pressures of governing a Kingdom, but to provide a prosperous future to each and every one of you. Someone who we can all look up to in times of trouble, with pride and honour.'

Jack couldn't help but smile as he looked across the auditorium at the multiple heads, nodding in agreement with his father's speech.

'Now, as much as I miss each and every one of you, I have made a life for myself in the homins world, where, despite this little adventure, my family and I are happy.'

James began making his way across the platform. 'Which is why, Mr Henry Xavier Gryphon Bagwell, is the only goblin I trust to lead this great Kingdom. He has proven in his most recent journey that his loyalty is unquestionable. He has the strength and determination to prevail, no matter how bleak the future looks.'

James's fingers danced in a circular motion as a radiant crown appeared in his right hand.

Although he willed it to stop, Henry could feel his cheeks getting hotter and hotter. He turned to James and spoke quietly. 'But I don't know how to be a king.'

'You will learn, and I will be here to support you, should you need me.' James said. 'This is something you must do.'

James placed the crown firmly on Henry's head. While the newly appointed king turned to face the exuberant crowd. Henry tried his best, but he couldn't restrain the enormous smile from spreading across his face.

James placed his hand on Henry's shoulder, and then edged himself away, allowing King Henry to take in the full hysteria of the elated crowd.

Henry looked over to Jack and Codie, who were also beaming from ear to ear. Henry mouthed the words 'thank you!' to the two boys.

James made his way towards his children and placed a gentle hand on each of their shoulders. 'It's time to go boys.'

Before either of the boys could begin to argue, the sight before them began to spin, the sound of the crowd grew faint and each of the two suns up above, merged into one.

The smiles on the boys faces quickly changed to frowns, as they realised they were no longer surrounded by ecstatic goblins, but were instead standing at the entrance to Lakewood Primary School.

A furious looking Ms Ratch turned to look at them, her foot tapping frantically against the concrete below. She was unsurprisingly wearing the same grey suit she had on yesterday. 'What time do you call this? You're over fifteen minutes late!'

'Apologies Ms Ratch,' James replied. 'Completely my fault. We had a bit of a heavy pillow morning today.'

Ms Ratch stood perfectly still, glowering at the three of them, eyebrows frowning angrily, arms folded, face like a smacked bum.

James knelt down and spoke to his children in a hushed tone. 'Listen boys, I will explain everything tonight, ok? I'm sorry we had to leave so quickly but if we'd left it another minute I think Ms Ratch might have exploded.' He looked over his shoulder at the livid teacher.

'What about Henry? Can we see him again?' Jack asked.

'Of course you can.'

'Does mum know who you are? I mean, that you're a prince?' Codie asked.

Ms Ratch cleared her throat and began tapping her foot even more frantically against the concrete.

James drew his children in close.

'Listen to me. I will explain everything tonight,' he said. 'Now you had better get a move on or I think Ms Ratch is going to turn into a goblin herself!'

The boys reluctantly agreed to wait until after school to have their questions answered. Each of them gave their father a fierce hug before being handed their schoolbags. James smiled down at the boys as he stood up tall on his prosthetics.

'We'll talk tonight. Hopefully everything will become a bit clearer. Until then, maybe don't mention your little journey to anyone in class. Don't want them thinking we're weird, do we?'

The brothers agreed, each giving their father one final hug, before heading past a furious Ms Ratch and into the school grounds.

That Night

Jack and Codie were waiting patiently on their living room sofa, Codie was sitting upright picking at a loose piece of thread from one of the cushions, while Jack was busying himself by counting the lumpy bits on the ceiling.

The silver clock hanging from the wall opposite the two boys was happily ticking away. The longer the children waited, the louder it seemed to become.

The children's mother wandered through to the living room, sitting down on the sofa at the opposite end of the room. Sallie was in her arms, smiling away at nothing in particular.

Tick-tock.

It felt as if time was standing still.

Tick-tock.

Mum started to give Sallie her bottle and the little girl sucked away happily.

Tick-tock.

The boy's mother had been a closed book ever since they had arrived home from school. Both Jack and Codie had tried to get information out of her, each of them had been told that they would need to wait until their father returned from work. This in all honesty, was very annoying, as both brothers were convinced that their mother could provide the answers they were so desperate for.

'How did you get on at school then?' Mum asked, breaking the silence, as she shifted Sallie into a more comfortable position.

Jack screwed his head away from the ceiling, having lost count. 'As riveting as ever.'

After the exhilarating adventure of the previous couple of days, school just didn't seem to cut it; it was so tedious. There was simply no excitement at school. Who wants to be learning about chimney sums, when you could be battling armies of Powries or scaling the impenetrable Wall of Segregation.

Codie jumped with excitement as a set of headlights lit up the entire living room. The moment they had been waiting for. Their father had finally returned from work.

The boys sat patiently and listened. They could hear the car being shut off, the door opening and then closing, before a set of footsteps grew louder up the garden path.

The front door swung open and their father stood in the doorway with a great smile on his face. He unfastened his black work jacket, plumped his briefcase down on the table and removed his polished leather shoes. He took a seat opposite the boys, next to the children's mother. The brothers continued to watch their father as he made some droll goo-goo gaga noises at Sallie.

After a moment, he turned to the boys and suggested something neither of them had anticipated.

'Right, are you two ready for bed?'

'WHAT!' Jack leapt off the sofa in frustration. 'We've been waiting all day for you to explain everything that happened. Do you think I'm going to be able to get to sleep now? How am I meant to go to school tomorrow not knowing what happened to Henry? What happened to the rest....'

Jack stopped himself. His father had a wide smile spread across his face.

The boy took a deep breath. 'You're messing with me, aren't you?'

'I'm sorry son, it's just so hard not to,' James chuckled, looking across at the boys' mother, who fixed him with a disapproving stare.

Their father sat up straight and cleared his throat.

'I'm sorry boys,' he said sincerely. 'Now, what do you want to know?'

Before Jack had a chance to speak, Codie butted in. 'Are we all goblins?'

James looked at their mother, then back at the children. 'No, you're not goblins.'

The children looked on, unsure.

'When I first came here, to this land, I didn't know anyone. I had no friends, no family – it was just me. It was difficult. After a while, I decided I needed a plan. The first thing I knew I need to do was to appear to be human.'

'It's pronounced homin, dad!' Jack corrected.

James laughed. 'Sorry son,' he said. 'Anyway, in order to appear homin, I had to make some cosmetic changes. And that started with a pair of prosthetic legs. Once I got my balance sorted, it opened up a whole new world to me. My next priority was to get a job. I got lucky too. Do you remember my boss Mr Dente?'

The children nodded. They had met Dad's boss on a few occasions in the past. Mr Dente was a pencil-thin man with a bushy grey moustache and a big heart. Although for someone in his profession, he had some of the worst teeth either of the children had ever seen.

'Well Mr Dente was looking for someone to help manage the finances at his dental practice and being the generous man he was, he offered to give me a job. That was when I met your mother and I won't gross you out too much but after many years of friendship, your mother and I began dating, we fell in love and then we found out Mum was going to have a baby.'

'Cool story,' said Jack, putting his index finger in his mouth and pretending to retch.

'Very funny,' Dad said.

'But none of this explains why you're a goblin and we're not?' said Codie.

'I was getting to that,' James said, as Sallie let out an enormous belch. 'You see, when two creatures love each other and decide to start a family, the children will always take after the more prominent species, which in our case, was homin. Only once has there been a goblin baby born from a homin and a goblin and, well let's just say, the baby turned out to be one of the worst, if not the worst goblin in history.'

'Worse than King Geerah?' Codie asked sounding amazed.

James looked at Amy, unsure how much to tell the boys.

Amy shook her head.

'Let's just say this goblin makes King Geerah look like fluffy kitten,' James said.

'So, we're never going to turn into goblins?' Jack asked, sounding slightly disappointed.

'I'm afraid not. I hope that's ok?'

'It's ok.'

'Although it would have been so cool to tell our friends that we were real live goblins.' Codie admitted.

'It's just as well really,' said James. 'Ain't neither of you two cut out for a shrink spurt.'

'A what?' said the boys together.

'A shrink spurt. You see, up until about the age of twelve, a homin child and a goblin are roughly the same size. Usually when a homin child reaches about thirteen they have a growth spurt, yes?'

The children nodded.

'Well it's kind of the opposite if you're a goblin. Instead of having a growth spurt, a goblin has a shrink spurt. And it's not just getting smaller that's the problem. Sickness bugs, uncontrollable temper tantrums, malediction - very nasty stuff, and it can go on for years - in some cases, forever. No, you two have had a lucky escape there, believe me.'

There was a brief moment of silence before Jack spoke again.

'You know when Henry was here, he...'

'Wow, wait a minute,' Mum said, sounding shocked. 'Henry was here?'

'Yes, he was here, erm...' Jack had unsurprisingly lost track. 'This morning.'

'I had no idea,' Mum confessed.

'Yes, during breakfast, but we kept him well hidden,' Codie said proudly.

'So that's why you two were in such a hurry to get back upstairs after breakfast? I did think it was strange why you two were being so... nice to each other.'

'Anyway,' Jack continued, desperate for more answers. 'When we went back upstairs after breakfast, we heard Henry talking to the Tempus Tarda. He never got the chance to tell us who he was talking to?'

Amy looked at her husband. James sighed.

'What intuitive children we have,' he said to his wife. 'Right, what do you know about the Tempus Tarda?' James asked.

'We know it belonged to a Kobold called Berke and that Geerah killed him and stole it for himself.'

James glanced at the boys' mother.

'It's better that they hear it from you James,' Amy said.

The boys' father relented. 'The Tempus Tarda was given to Berke's great-great-grandfather, Titus. Legend has it that Titus assisted Argon in the creation of the Kingdom. Titus worked night and day for an entire year, resting for only three hours each night. Once the Kingdom was complete, Argon told Titus that, for his efforts, he would ensure that his family would each be rewarded with long and happy lives. True to his word, Titus and his wife, Alma, both lived happy and untroubled lives. Many decades later however, Alma became very ill and died. Titus was left inconsolable and eventually died himself. Before he perished however, he picked his successor to rule the Kingdom. Throughout history, Kobolds invariably stuck with their own kind. That particular rule was turned on its head when Titus picked his successor, his best friend, a goblin, to be king. Can you guess who his best friend was?'

'I know!' Codie shouted. 'It was your dad, it was King Gola, wasn't it?'

'Correct!' James said. 'When Alma died, Argon realised how upset Titus was, and he created the Tempus Tarda.'

'But what does it do?' Codie asked, almost falling off his seat.

'Among other powers the Tempus Tarda possesses, it allows the spirits of both Alma and Titus to join together, thus giving Titus, the Kobold who helped Argon, a very powerful gift - the gift of eternal love.

'So that's why the Tempus Tarda was so important to the Kobolds?' Jack asked. 'It was a gift from Argon.'

'Correct! The Kobolds regard Titus as a very important figure in their history and believe in the powers of the Tempus Tarda, they even pray to it - three times a day. They use it in times of trouble, when they're searching for answers. Some Kobolds believe it can even produce miracles. This is exactly the reason Geerah was destined to fail the moment he killed Berke and stole the Tempus Tarda for himself.'

The room fell silent as the children processed this new information. Sallie gurgling away in her mum's arms broke the silence.

'So how did Henry end up with the Tempus Tarda in the first place and how did he know to come here?' Jack asked.

James thought for a moment. 'Well that I can't answer. I can only presume Henry had taken all he could and decided to do something about it. As for how he ended up here, again I'm not sure; perhaps the Tempus Tarda led him here? Trying to understand the will of the Tempus Tarda is like attempting to fit the entire Atlantic Ocean in a teacup!'

The brothers seemed confused at this.

'Don't dwell on it children,' their mother said. 'It won't do you any good.'

James looked at his watchless wrist, 'Right, it's getting late you two, up to bed. Let's face it you've had a busy day.'

The boys were exhausted and didn't put up much of a fight. They kissed their mother and sister goodnight, before making their way up the stairs.

All through the process of putting their pyjamas on and brushing their teeth, the questions came thick and fast.

'How old was Argon?' Jack asked.

'How did Henry's parents die?' Codie queried.

'Why haven't you gone back to the Kingdom until now?'

As James tucked the boys into their beds, he explained that no one knew how old Argon was, although if he had to guess he would have estimated somewhere in the region of 500. Henry's parents had been caught up in a tragic explosion when he was only thirteen, leaving the goblin alone in the world. His auntie Anne had stepped in to look after the adolescent goblin.

Finally, James had explained that not long after he'd fled the Kingdom he had met and fell in love with the children's mother. Had it not been for his children venturing to the Kingdom with Henry, he probably would never have returned.

'Perhaps,' said James. 'That's the reason why Henry turned up here.

'Are you glad you went back?' asked Jack mid-yawn.

'I am,' confessed James. 'For too long, I've tried to close myself off from my past life, convince myself that it didn't happen. Yet returning after all this time has made me realise something.'

'What?' asked Codie.

'That it all happened for a reason,' James said simply. 'I loved my father very much, but had it not been for the fact that Geerah killed him, I would never have left the Kingdom. I would never have met your mother and we would never have had three beautiful children.'

James let out a great, weary yawn.

'Right boys, it's very late. If you're half as tired as I am, you must be exhausted. 'Last question, make it a good one.'

Within a heartbeat both Jack and Codie asked simultaneously. 'Will we ever see Henry again?'

James chuckled. 'Of course!'

'But when can we see him?' Codie challenged.

'I suspect Henry will be very busy running a Kingdom, and you two will be busy at school over the coming weeks. Tell you what, it's only a few weeks until school breaks up for the Christmas holidays. Why don't we all go and visit Henry in the Kingdom over Christmas?'

'Do you mean it?' Jack asked, springing up in bed, any chance of sleep momentarily disappearing.

Codie sat up in bed too. 'But I thought homin children weren't allowed in the Kingdom?'

'True,' James agreed. 'That *was* the rule when Geerah was in charge, but I suspect our new King will be somewhat more lenient.'

James kissed both of his children on the forehead.

'Goodnight Jack. Goodnight Codie.'

'Good night dad,' yawned each of the boys.

James closed the boys' bedroom door until all was still and dark, except for a small nightlight in the corner of the room.

The chubby goblin in the wardrobe smiled to himself and whispered. 'Good night James.'